SURVIVAL STRATEGIES OF THE ALMOST BRAVE

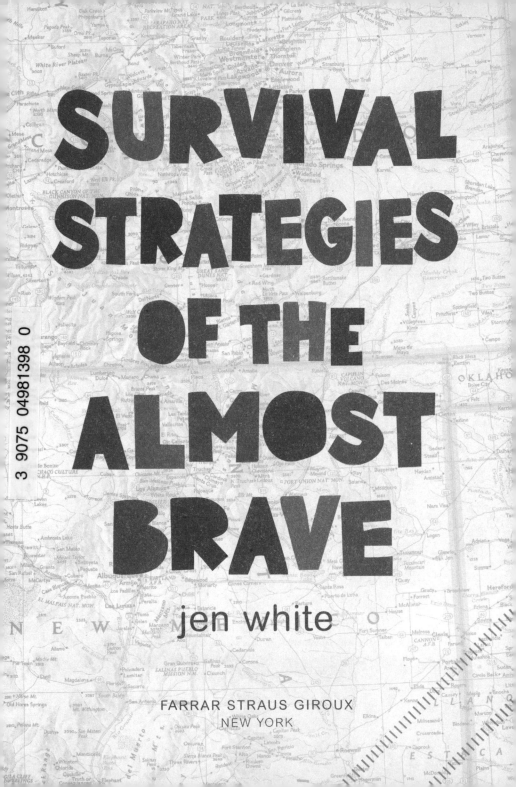

SURVIVAL STRATEGIES OF THE ALMOST BRAVE

jen white

FARRAR STRAUS GIROUX
NEW YORK

Farrar Straus Giroux Books for Young Readers
175 Fifth Avenue, New York 10010

Printed in the United States of America by R. R. Donnelley
& Sons Company, Harrisonburg, Virginia
Designed by Elizabeth H. Clark
First edition, 2015

1 3 5 7 9 10 8 6 4 2

macteenbooks.com

Library of Congress Cataloging-in-Publication Data
White, Jen.
    Survival strategies of the almost brave / Jen White.
        pages cm
    Summary: Soon after their mother's sudden death in San Diego, Liberty, twelve,
and Billie, eight, are abandoned at an Arizona gas station by the father they barely
know and Liberty must find a way to keep them together and safe until either Dad
returns or they can contact Julie, their mother's best friend.
    ISBN 978-0-374-30084-5 (hardback)
    ISBN 978-0-374-30085-2 (e-book)
    [1. Abandoned children—Fiction. 2. Sisters—Fiction. 3. Single-parent
families—Fiction. 4. Fathers and daughters—Fiction. 5. Survival—Fiction.]
I. Title.

PZ7.1.W445Sur 2015
[Fic]—dc23
                                                                2014040665

Farrar Straus Giroux Books for Young Readers may be purchased for business or
promotional use. For information on bulk purchases please contact Macmillan
Corporate and Premium Sales Department at (800) 221-7945 x5442 or
by email at specialmarkets@macmillan.com.

COLORADO
NEW MEXICO
OKLAHO
LLANO
ESTACA
Colorado Springs
Denver
Pueblo
Albuquerque
Santa Fe

For Adam

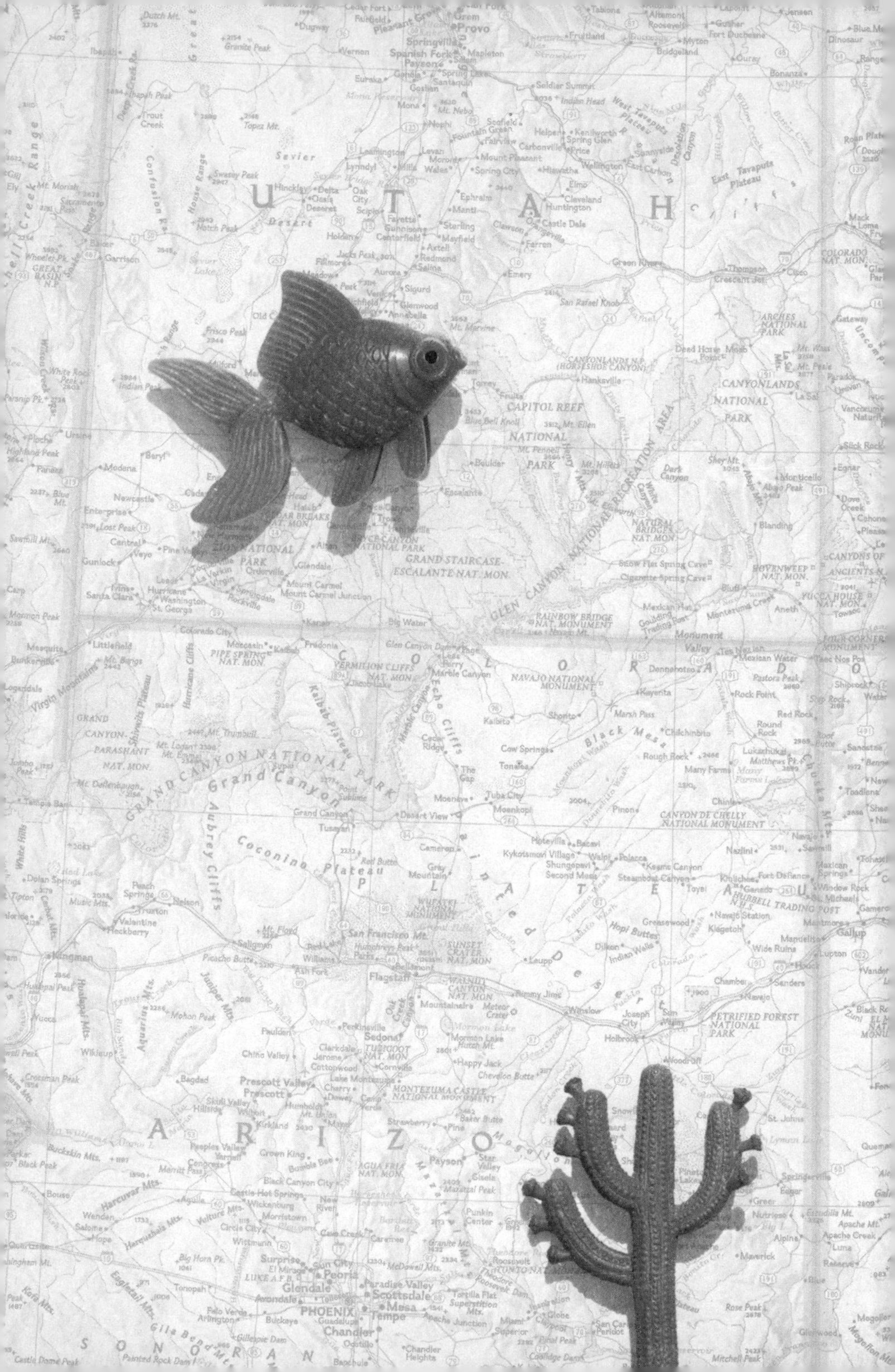

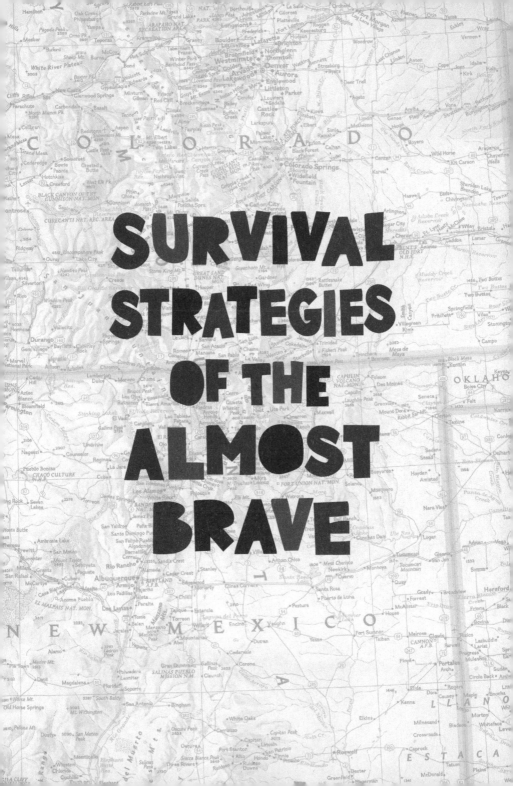

SURVIVAL STRATEGIES OF THE ALMOST BRAVE

U T A H
A R I Z O N A
C O L O R A D O
P L A T E A U
S O N O R A N
CAPITOL REEF NATIONAL PARK
CANYONLANDS NATIONAL PARK
ARCHES NATIONAL PARK
BRYCE CANYON NATIONAL PARK
ZION NATIONAL PARK
GRAND STAIRCASE-ESCALANTE NAT. MON.
GLEN CANYON NATIONAL RECREATION AREA
RAINBOW BRIDGE NAT. MONUMENT
NAVAJO NATIONAL MONUMENT
CANYON DE CHELLY NATIONAL MONUMENT
PETRIFIED FOREST NATIONAL PARK
SUNSET CRATER NAT. MON.
WALNUT CANYON NAT. MON.
MONTEZUMA CASTLE NATIONAL MONUMENT
TUZIGOOT NAT. MON.
TONTO NAT. MONUMENT
Provo
Flagstaff
Prescott
Sedona
Payson
PHOENIX
Scottsdale
Mesa
Tempe
Glendale
Chandler
Kingman
Monument Valley
Green River
Moab
Mogollon Rim
Painted Desert

Survival Strategy #1:
FAKE IT

FAKE IT.

That's definitely number one in my notebook. All people do it. Faking it could save your life.

Just then, I was faking it. Writing in my notebook, like I had a purpose. A reason for being here. Like I had all the time in the world to sit outside this sun-scorched gas station, waiting. I should have known better. All my natural instincts told me not to trust him.

"Where's Daddy?" Billie asked. At eight, she was four years younger than me and forever wishing he would turn into the dream dad she'd always hoped for. So all right, we had *both* hoped for. But after everything that had happened, now I knew better. Even if I wanted to cry (and I'm not saying I did), I couldn't let Billie see me.

Now I was just angry. Angry like the sun that burned a hole in the desert sky, so hot and bright, it might just eat us up.

"Liberty, where is he?" whispered Billie, a crease of dirt, like a lightning bolt, slashed across her swollen cheek. I reached for it, but she shrugged me away.

"I don't know. Don't worry, he's coming back," I said, trying to hide my fear and convince both of us he *was* coming back. What else could we do but sit on the curb and wait?

I patted Billie's hair and forced a smile. "He's coming." I hated faking it with her, even though sometimes I couldn't help it.

"What about this morning?" she choked out. The whites of her eyes were slippery with tears. "It was an accident."

"He knows that, Billie. Don't worry. Come sit with me." I curled my arm over her back, nothing but angles and lines, and willed my tears to return to their ducts. Stupid tears; they would *not* scare Billie.

"I'm hot," she said, pushing free of me. She wandered toward the shade over near the gas pumps.

A car rolled past the gas station, and Billie stood on her tippy-toes to see over the JIFFY CO. GAS STATION sign.

A brown Jeep.

Not our camper. Were we in Arizona? This morning

we had been in Arizona—the Grand Canyon State (at least that's what the sign had said)—but one of the weird things about living in a camper is that you can fall asleep in one state, wake up in another, and not even know.

Dad stopped here at the Jiffy Co. to fill up over an hour ago. Billie and me went inside to use the bathroom. When we came out, he was gone. Already, we had been waiting too long. My heart bumped.

I tried to distract my brain and opened my notebook again, scanning the pages of animal facts. Already, I felt better. The only thing to do now was to be purely logical, and wait. I could do that. I could do that for Billie.

From where we sat on the curb, the glass on the gas station door looked smudged with countless sweaty hands. It hadn't opened in a while. Three whole cars had creaked across the gravel road and deposited themselves in front of the gas pumps, shiny with oil.

A million bat wings beat against the lining of my stomach. I might throw up.

Stop it, Liberty. Facts only.

Did you know a cow has four stomachs? I saw that on Animal Planet, back before—

No.

I balanced my notebook on the tips of my knees.

Another car drove past.

I scooched around on the curb to the side of the

cinder-block building, keeping my eye on Billie. What had Mom always said? *You're in charge, Liberty.* Mom hadn't had a brother or a sister, but she'd always wanted one. That's why she had two children, so Billie and me would have each other. Sisters forever. But being the oldest can be hard. Billie didn't always appreciate everything I knew.

Mom took it for granted that I did what I should. *Twelve going on twenty-one,* she had said. But what she didn't realize was that I was always responsible because I had to be. At least, almost always.

A line of ants crawled over a potato chip from the bag I bought from the vending machine after Dad left, what felt like years ago. I wrote in my notebook:

1. Ants, red.
2. Playing follow the leader.
3. Never alone. Always together.
4. Brave.

I didn't know what my hypothesis was about ants yet, but they looked like good friends. Maybe a family.

Did ants fake it?

I patted the cover of my notebook. It was still new and shiny in some places, but worn around the edges. It felt smooth and soft. Notebooks were good. Something to touch and hold. I wrote everything in my notebook because every good scientist had important observations. I wasn't a scientist yet, but I was going to be one someday.

I opened my book and read an entry in the middle from about six months ago—when Mom took Billie and me to the aquarium in La Jolla. The Birch Aquarium was, by far, my favorite place.

Spotted Wobbegong Sharks.
Dive and Live Feeding Schedule:
Mondays 10:00 a.m. and 12:00 p.m.

I'd begged Mom to take me back to watch the live dive. I couldn't believe someone could actually get into the shark tank and feed them. Mom said *maybe.* Maybe we could go next week. But I never saw those sharks again.

I shut my book. I didn't want to think about sharks, either. So I watched the ants. Hundreds of little skinny ant arms grabbed the chip and dragged it toward the gash in the asphalt parking lot, just as the sun reached its highest point in the sky.

A truck (the fourth one we'd seen) pulled into the gas station with a low, squeaky whine. Blue, dusty, ancient. An old man with a ponytail and a huge belt buckle got out and stared at us. Billie ran over and crouched behind me. My heart vibrated. But then I remembered, I was faking it. I was supposed to scare off potential predators.

Go away.

A bearded dragon has a chin full of spiky armor it uses to intimidate. It inflates its body, opens its mouth, and puffs out its lethal throat. Then the attacker thinks twice about messing with that lizard.

I took a deep breath, stood as tall as I could, and stared right back at the man—without blinking. He turned, opened the door, and went inside.

That's right. Go inside and buy your gas. Me? I haven't a problem in the world. I stood tall in front of Billie and shaded my eyes from the hot desert sun.

Billie poked her head out from behind me. "You still watching for Dad?" she asked.

I pulled her hair back to get a look at her cheek, but she jerked away.

"He'll be back. I know it. He'll be back for us," she said.

Billie didn't know anything.

But still, she was my baby sister. Stringy white hair, dark blue eyes. Pure gold. That's what she was. Ever since Mom died, Billie reminded me of pure gold, not that fake kind you buy as a souvenir in old tourist mining towns, or mixed in with the semiprecious stones at an Indian gift shop. The real thing, fourteen karat.

After living in a camper for the past two months, San Diego felt light-years away. Like we had slipped through a crack in the atmosphere and dipped ourselves into this strange summer, sticky with newness. And still after everything, we were alone. Just the two of us roasting in clay on this quiet, dusty road.

The JIFFY CO. GAS STATION sign swayed and creaked. It didn't matter how long I sat here writing in my notebook, faking it—he wasn't coming back.

I had to fix it.

But how?

Survival Strategy #2:
ACT NORMAL

SO FAR MY PLAN WAS TO FAKE IT, OF COURSE. But then what?

1. Act normal.
2. Take care of Billie.

I could do those two things.

"Billie!" I yelled. "Quit picking your nose."

She jumped.

"Get in the shade! You're turning red like a lobster."

Heat radiated from the blacktop, making the gas pumps look all wiggly. Billie ignored me. Her black sparkly flip-flops might melt right into the asphalt. Then she turned and looked me full in the face, her blue eyes deep and solemn, like a deer I'd seen once on the Discovery Channel.

Billie walked toward me, bunching the extra material of her sweatshirt up into her hands, like she was holding a ball.

"Don't you have a T-shirt under that?"

She shook her head. A single trickle of sweat crept down her face. She pushed it away with the back of her hand.

"Will you please come sit in the shade, away from that window?" I asked. I was sitting on the left side of the gas station so prying eyes couldn't see us. So far, we were lucky that the creepy gas station attendant hadn't come out asking any questions. We had been inside twice—once to use the bathroom and once to look for Dad—and I didn't want to push our luck.

"Where'd he go?" she asked.

That was something I could hardly think about.

Yesterday he said we were on our way to Four Corners, the only place in the United States where you could stand in four states at once. Utah. Colorado. New Mexico. Arizona. Actually, I really wanted to do that. It seemed almost to defy science; it shouldn't be possible to be in four places at once. But in Four Corners you could be—like magic, but provable. Now, after what happened this morning, even if Dad did come back, I wouldn't go with him. But I couldn't tell Billie that.

Act normal.

"He probably just went to get . . . to get . . ." I stopped.

"To get ice cream!" Billie finished. "It's so hot that Dad went to get us ice cream."

I nodded. Ice cream right now sounded good, real good. And the lie seemed easier than the truth. I almost convinced myself we had nothing to worry about. We were just two sisters waiting at a gas station for our dad to bring us a scoop of triple fudge ice cream. That's the thing about faking it: it's pretty easy to do if you're good at it. But I knew I was just pretending, because it didn't look like there was a store for miles.

We were surrounded by miles of emptiness—and my brain really wanted to panic. But an animal that panics is as good as dead. Like a deer at night, blinded by headlights. Frozen and then—*bam.* How many animals had I seen busted along the side of the road over the past two months? I couldn't count. Trust me, panic is not your friend. I pushed the fear back into the tiny crack in my head where it lived and tried to think about ants, or deer, or anything else.

"Knock, knock," Billie said.

Jokes were our thing. We used them to pass time while Dad searched for the perfect shot.

"Liberty! *Knock, knock.*"

"Who's there?"

"Ice cream."

My stomach grumbled. "Ice cream who?"

"Ice cream when I see your underwear!" She laughed like it was the funniest joke she'd ever heard, even though we'd recited it at least one hundred times.

"Get it? I scream."

"Yeah, I get it. That's a good one, Billie."

The door to the gas station opened. The old man came back out. He turned and looked at us. "Afternoon," he said, tipping his hat.

He seemed nicer now. Should I say something? Maybe he could help us. His truck door creaked open, he paused for a second, stared at us, and then . . . it was too late. He slammed the door and drove away. I glared at his bumper, wishing I had an invisible string to attach to it so he could drag us along.

The desert sand rolled around us like giant waves in the ocean. Up and down. Down and up. I had never seen red sand in person before, until Dad came and got us. At first it had seemed pretty, but now, being left in it, it felt like being lost at sea—a red sea made out of sand.

Survival Strategy #3:
BLUE SKIES DO NOT MEAN HAPPINESS

THE LAST TIME I SAW THE OCEAN, WE'D sprinkled Mom's ashes across the water. Our boat had bounced on top, like how the fish food bounced after I fed our goldfish, George and Martha. And I had started to feel a little sick. And it had only been nine days since Mom had died. And maybe I didn't want to believe it was all true.

So I'd stopped watching the waves roll up and down, and instead I looked at the sky. The sun glowed bright against the blue with little white sheep clouds floating everywhere. Little lost sheep clouds. It was a perfect beach day. Mom's funeral on the best beach day ever.

Julie had said, "You need a bucket, Liberty?"

I nodded.

"Joe. You have a bucket around here?"

The man named Joe driving the boat shook his head and pointed to the water. I couldn't throw up in there because that's where Mom was going. And I didn't even know this man Joe, who Julie said she paid to take us out in the ocean so Mom could be "put to rest" where she'd always wanted to be resting.

I didn't know Mom always wanted to rest in the ocean. I thought she always wanted to be with us.

But Julie said Mom *did* want to be resting in the ocean.

And since my grandma and grandpa were dead before I was ever alive and the only other family we had was Dad and we didn't know where he was, I had to listen to Julie. Because:

1. She was Mom's boss at work.
2. She was our neighbor.
3. She was Mom's best friend.

So Julie said what Billie and me had to do.

Which you would think would be okay because at Julie's condo she had a lot of candy. *A lot.* Not old, stale butterscotches, but jars of *candy*—the good kind, like M&M's, and Twix, and Starburst, and even some that I didn't recognize from Canada, like Coffee Crisps, and Sweet Maries (Billie liked those), and Wunderbars, all stuffed into jars across her kitchen counter. I'm sure all that candy wasn't good for her and that's probably why she was kind of fat, but what was I supposed to say about that?

Billie and me always liked the candy, but I didn't think just because she gave us candy, and took us to SeaWorld once, she should be the boss of us. But she was, because there was no one else who wanted two sisters to live with them for always.

At our condo, I'm-Sorry-You're-Dead flowers from Mom's friends at the hospital lined our island in the kitchen. My favorites were the purple snapdragons from Dr. Hammond, Mom's onetime (I think not-divorced) boyfriend. She didn't date him long but I liked the flowers he sent. She said dating with kids was too complicated. Once at the grocery store Mom showed me how if you squeeze snapdragons on their sides, their mouths open up like baby birds'. Snapdragons were my favorite talking flower.

Joe stopped the boat right next to an old buoy because he said the waves were getting rough. Seagulls stared at us with their give-us-some-food eyes.

Julie said, "That's far enough." And she handed me a big vase with cats on it.

"Mom doesn't like cats," said Billie.

I nodded. It was true. She didn't. Allergic.

Julie had two cats named Snickers and Runts. They

were very fat and picky and ate only tuna out of a can. Before Mom died, I cat-sat for them twice when Julie went to Canada to visit her brother.

"Of course she does, sweetie," said Julie, patting Billie on the top of her head.

"No, she doesn't. She's allergic," I said.

"Well, these aren't real cats. And we're not leaving the urn. Just your mom's ashes," she said, taking off the lid.

Billie and me peered inside. It couldn't be Mom. It looked like dirt.

"I thought she would be pink," said Billie. "Mom loves pink."

Julie wasn't listening. Instead she was staring out at the ocean like she might cry. Then she pulled a paper out of her pocket and read a poem about flowers and clouds and heaven.

And I took a handful of what-was-Mom-and-looked-like-dirt-but-felt-soft-and-slippery and sprinkled it across the water. Billie didn't want to touch it. And really, I didn't, either. But Julie told me to.

So I did.

Then Julie wiped tears from her eyes and emptied the rest of the vase right there into the Pacific Ocean. And Billie cried, too. But I didn't. Not yet.

Because it didn't seem right. How could we be here without her?

The waves went up and down, up and down, and carried Mom out to sea. And instead of wondering about Mom, I wondered what the fish were thinking. Was there a spotted wobbegong shark down there? Did he notice anything different about the specks of dust floating down to the ocean floor? Did he know those specks were my mom?

I didn't like to think about that.

Now, sitting here at the gas station, it was almost three months since we had put Mom in the ocean. I kept track of it in my notebook. And after that day everything changed. Julie found Dad's old address in Mom's papers. I never knew Mom had an old address—like a treasure map—that told us where to find him. When I'd asked where he was before, Mom had always said he was traveling or she didn't know where to find him. But Julie said the person who lived at that old address had Dad's phone number.

So a few weeks after Mom's funeral, on the day Julie volunteered at the free walk-in clinic, she called him.

She said Dad was sad to hear about Mom. And that he would come and get us, even though we hadn't seen him since I was six years old. She didn't say what Dad had said about Billie or me. She just said that he was coming and that he couldn't wait.

Really?

Probably that was just Julie being enthusiastic. But still, it made me wonder about everything Mom had ever told me about Dad, especially if she had the old-address-treasure-map and never told us. Mostly, it made me wonder what it would be like to have a real flesh-and-bone kind of dad, like I had always wished for when I sometimes looked at the three pictures I had of him.

Maybe he was like Suzanne Gomez's firefighter dad. He seemed really nice, even though she was bratty. He came to our class once to talk about fire safety. She said he coached her soccer team, and he made the best chocolate chip pancakes, and he took her to McDonald's for no special reason at all. Mom never took us to McDonald's. Having a dad around was probably pretty awesome.

Julie had said he'd take us for sure for the summer and probably, if everything went well, then he would have us for always. Didn't he already know he wanted us? Almost all of me knew I wanted him. Isn't that what kids are supposed to do? Be with their dads for always?

But now, looking at the empty road, that was our answer, wasn't it? He was gone. And we were here.

Billie sighed. "I'm bored."

"I know," I said. "Tell me a joke."

She shook her head. "I want to go home."

I knew she meant San Diego. Billie usually never talked

about home, but after what had happened this morning, of course she wanted to go home.

Before Mom died we had only ever lived in San Diego. And Billie and me had never been anywhere. But Dad had been everywhere because he was a photographer. He'd been to Africa and China and Brazil and the Amazon and I think Puerto Rico, and probably lots of places I didn't even know. So I watched *Hunter and Hunted* every day on NatGeo because Mom said Dad took pictures for *National Geographic* magazine. And what if he ever came to visit us? We would need something to talk about, right?

So now I knew a lot about animals; I mean, I knew *a lot*.

Animals are important, like, essential to the human life cycle and the environment; at least that's what my sixth grade teacher, Mrs. Mortensen, told me. She said the world would be nothing without the animal kingdom. So that really made sense to me about Dad and why he was gone. Because why would he leave us unless he was doing something really important?

Survival Strategy #4:
WATCH OUT FOR PREDATORS

AN OLD BURNED-OUT CAR SAT A FEW hundred feet from the gas station. My watch said 1:34. The car looked like a gutted fish. Like the ones we saw with Julie lying in a row at the pier right before we scattered Mom's ashes. That day, there were a lot of fishermen and a lot of dead fish.

In the desert there are no fish, of course. Only rattlesnakes or other dangerous things like spiders, and lizards, and scorpions. In the desert you have to be careful; predators could easily turn into prey.

A blue car pulled into the gas station. The engine clicked off, but no one got out. The car just sat.

Billie came and stood by me.

For a second I began to worry. Could it be Dad in a different car? Had the camper broken down?

The door creaked open slowly, so slowly that I could probably count to a million, and then I saw a tip of a shoe. A lavender shoe so shiny that the sun seemed to glow right from the tip. And then purple nubby pants. And finally, a whole body of a person so skinny she might blow away like a plastic bag, but the wind didn't exist here, so she stayed put. A cigarette dangled from her lips, and her face was covered in miles of wrinkles that could stretch all the way back to the ocean, I bet. She shielded her eyes from the sun. Maybe she was nocturnal.

"What?" she croaked into the crispy fried air. "Speak up, I can't hear you."

I slunk closer to the cinder blocks and the ice machine, pulling Billie with me.

The Lavender Lady leaned back into her car, adjusting something, and then coughed. "Now it's on. What?" Her neck stretched farther into the car. "I know!" The door slammed so hard, my fillings rattled.

She crossed the gravel parking lot like a slug on the sidewalk after an early morning rain, and silently slipped through the gas station door with a trail of cigarette smoke following her.

The car window was too shaded to get a good look inside. Who had the Lavender Lady been talking to?

I reached into my pocket and felt something squish. I pulled out a smashed Twinkie I got from the camper this morning, still in its wrapper.

"Billie," I said, holding it up.

She smiled.

"Here." I shoved it into her hands. But before she could enjoy it, the gas station door slammed open. I turned. It was the creepy guy who worked inside.

He walked slowly, his hands tucked into his pockets. And for a second he paused and stared out at the gas pumps, but then he turned and headed straight toward us.

"Whatcha kids doing?" he asked. The glare off his bald head was so bright, I squinted and shaded my eyes with my hand. "I seen you out here. Where's your mom?"

I flinched; just hearing that greasy man ask about Mom made my head hurt. But I put on my most responsible voice and said, "Our dad will be back any minute. He just went to get . . ."

I hesitated.

"Ice cream," Billie said. She circled her small arms around my waist. Since Mom died, she usually only ever talked to me.

"Shush," I said, elbowing her.

She gripped me tighter.

"Ice cream?"

"Yes, ice cream." I tried not to look at Shiny Head's eyes and just concentrated on the blue thread that was hanging from the patch above his front pocket that said VERN.

"Well, your daddy ain't going to find any ice cream 'round here."

He put his leathery hand on his hip and gazed down the road as the ice machine switched on. It coughed and hummed.

"All right, thank you. We're okay."

He stood and stared. My back felt all crawly.

I chanted in my head: *Go away.*

Once I saw a lady on TV control minds just by chanting what she wished for inside her head over and over again. I tried it, and sometimes it worked, like when I didn't want Billie to eat the last Rolo.

It could work now.

Go away.

Go away.

Go away.

Billie squeezed my waist harder.

"Unless he went to Monticello," he said slowly. "That where he went?"

"Yep. That's it. Should be back any minute. We're fine. Thank you, sir," I said, pulling Billie around the corner where the ice machine sat, fat and heavy.

"Hold up," said Shiny Head, following us. He pulled on the blue thread, wrapping it tight around his finger. "Why didn't your dad take you with him?"

I backed up.

He stopped pulling and put his hands back in his deep pockets, like maybe he was harmless, like a puppy dog.

Then his eyes narrowed.

"Don't worry," he said, licking the sweat off his upper lip. "I'll help you girls." He lowered his voice and leaned in. "Just tell me what kind of trouble you're in." His breath felt heavy on my face and smelled like something dead.

Go away.

I grabbed Billie's hand and squeezed it hard.

Do it. Do it, Billie. Fake it, fake it right now.

Our eyes locked for a moment, and then . . . she nodded. After all this time, we really didn't need to speak; we understood each other.

"Liberty, I don't feel so good," moaned Billie. "I don't feel good at all." She clutched her stomach and bowed forward like she was looking at her flip-flops.

"Carsick," I said too loud, looking past Shiny Head's shoulders. "My sister's carsick."

Fake car sickness had saved us when we needed to stop for food and Dad didn't want Billie to barf in the camper.

"Here it comes," shouted Billie, her big eyes glassy, hand over her mouth.

Shiny Head jerked back, his nose scrunched up like he'd stepped in dog poop.

I pushed past him and dragged moaning Billie inside, into the gas station, through the shop and then into the bathroom.

We locked the door behind us. The bathroom sucked us in, like it was taking one big deep breath. One hot, stinky breath. I knelt down next to the door and listened for Shiny Head. My knees stuck to the floor. Toilet paper snakes coiled around the sink, ready to strike.

Billie slid down next to me and breathed out slow and long, like a balloon deflating. We sat there waiting for something. Just waiting.

Where was Dad?

Deep inside, I felt cold. Like the panic seeped out of the cramped crease inside my brain and dripped slowly into my bloodstream.

Survival Strategy #5:
HIBERNATE

"DON'T YOU LOCK ME OUT!" YELLED SHINY
Head. His hand slapped at the door, the wood bouncing
with each smack.

"As soon as I find my keys, you'll be sorry," he growled.
His footsteps faded away.

Please, keys, stay hidden. Hibernate for life.

Billie smiled. Then she laughed, kind of crazy-like.
"Did you see his face when I hunched over? He thought
I was going to spew all over his nasty shoes."

"Shh," I said, grabbing her hand. It was shaking.

"Spew," she said smiling. "Spew on his shoe."

She covered her mouth and laughed like she'd just
heard the funniest knock-knock joke in the world.

I smiled, uneasy. "Shh."

Then Billie's eyes got big and she really did throw up, all over the floor and her sparkly flip-flops. I dragged her over to the toilet, grabbed some paper towels, and tried to clean her off. I threw her flip-flops into the sink.

Billie began to cry. And when she cried, I guessed it was all right for me to cry, too.

I cried because Shiny Head was ugly and scary. I cried because the bathroom stank like a Porta-Potty. And I cried for other important things, like:

1. Mom was floating in the ocean.
2. Dad was gone.
3. We were lost and alone.

"Where's Daddy?" asked Billie, sniffing real loud and clinging to my neck like she was a baby sloth and I was her mama. Baby sloths and their mamas don't ever like to be separated. She closed her eyes as I smoothed the hair on top of her head.

"Don't worry, Billie. I'm here. I'm not going to let you go." And this time, I wasn't faking it.

My hair wound around my sticky neck. I pulled it loose, slipped it back into a ponytail, and sat up straight. Billie curled into herself on the tile floor, just like a hermit crab.

She had vomit in her hair. And on her sweatshirt.

Thump. Thump. Thump.

He was back. The door shook with each pound. "Hey. Hey, you in there!"

The blood rushed to my head as I stood and grabbed on to the sink. I guess he hadn't found his keys.

He pounded again. "I've called the sheriff!"

The sheriff. Even I knew nothing good happened when someone called the sheriff. I could still remember the two uniformed policemen who stood on our front step the day Mom died. No policemen—no sheriffs. Nothing but bad stuff came from them.

"Billie!" I said, nudging her with my tennis shoe. "Get up!"

Billie rubbed her eyes. They were red and puffy from all the crying, and toilet paper stuck to her sweaty cheek.

"Here," I said, kneeling down. "Come rinse your mouth out." Her breath was horrible.

She sat up, pulling on the arm of her sweatshirt. "Is it Dad?"

"No," I said, putting my ear to the door. I thought Shiny Head had left.

I stared at the cracked tiles on the floor. Mom would have never done this to us.

Billie whispered, "When Daddy comes back, I'm going to show him how good I can be. If we're really good, then he'll keep us."

Was that why he left? Because we were bad?

I shook off her words and stood up. "We *are* good."

Billie's cheek was turning a weird purple color. I could never forgive Dad for that cheek.

I tried to pull her up. "Come on, let's go." The toilet paper on her face waggled as she silently shook her head. Her feet were still bare. The black sparkly flip-flops sat wet and shiny in the sink.

I picked the toilet paper off, and Billie snapped out of her trance.

"I'm not leaving until Dad comes," she said.

I folded my arms, ready for a fight. Queen Billie. Mom always called her Queen Billie when she got stubborn.

"We can't sit here all day."

Billie stuck out her chin. "I'm not leaving."

"Billie!" I was hot and tired. "Didn't you hear that guy? He said he's calling the sheriff! We've got to get out of here."

Billie's stone face crumpled. "The sheriff?" Tears leaked out of her eyes. "Is he taking us to jail?"

I didn't want to scare her. I took her hand and pulled her up. "No, no. Stop it. Stop crying, okay?" Billie wiped her tears with the back of her hand. "No one's going to jail," I said.

At least we weren't. But what about Dad?

What if Julie didn't want us? Then where would we

go? To a foster home or an orphanage? I'd watched the news. Nobody loves you there. And what if they took Billie away from me?

No, my brain could hardly think the thought. Living with Dad was bad, but at least we were together. Billie and I had to stay together. I wasn't going to talk to any sheriff. For now, I would take care of us. I could do it. Not for the first time, I wished Mom had let me get a cell phone. But that didn't matter now. I could just find a phone and call Julie. I had her phone number. She would come and get us. Then everything would be all right.

"Let's go."

Billie still looked worried.

"Hey," I said, trying to make my voice sound hopeful. "Maybe Dad's outside. Maybe he came back and he's waiting for us with ice cream."

She stood up and grabbed the doorknob. "I didn't think about that."

"Wait!" I said, pulling her hand off. "We just can't leave. We have to plan."

"Why do we need a plan if Dad's outside?"

I lowered my voice. "Because of the sheriff. Do you want Dad to get into trouble?"

Billie's eyes filled with tears again. "No. I don't want Dad to get in trouble."

"Okay, just let me think."

Strategy. I needed a survival strategy. I reached for my notebook in my back pocket. But it was *gone*. Maybe I left it in the dirt by the ice machine. My heart flipped. I had to get it back.

What do animals do when they're cornered? They fight. But what could we do to a sheriff?

Billie looked at me, waiting.

"We can't let that Shiny Head gas station guy see us."

Billie nodded so hard, it looked like her head might roll off.

"And we're going to find Dad," she said.

"Yes, we'll look for Dad," I said, even though I was pretty sure he wasn't coming back.

Think. Think. Think.

I remembered a *Hunter and Hunted* episode where a snake had a family of prairie dogs cornered. The snake slithered closer, looking for lunch, when suddenly the prairie dogs charged, all of them running every which way. The snake didn't know which one to attack, so it went home hungry.

That's what we were going to do. Break it up.

I grabbed Billie's hands and squeezed them. They were soft and warm. I loved those hands—hands just like mine, just like Mom's.

She looked at me. "Tell me, Liberty. Tell me the plan. I can do it."

Survival Strategy #6:
FIGHT OR FLIGHT

I CRACKED OPEN THE BATHROOM DOOR. The gas station seemed empty. Dusty cans of motor oil stared back at me from their shelves. No Shiny Head. The snake was hiding . . . at least for now.

I turned to Billie. "Ready?"

"Ready."

I inched the door open. The hinges let out a squeal. Since being on the road with Dad, I knew a lot about gas stations, and truck stops, and gas stations attached to truck stops. This gas station was gross. Grosser than most.

I peeked around the corner and looked to the front. Boxes of car parts and metal cans lined the walls. The cash register counter was empty except for a plastic bin of Bubble Yum, and behind it was a row of windows so dirty, I couldn't see out. A lonely fan sputtered and choked above the front door.

I licked my cracked lips.

"Shh." I motioned to Billie. Her eyes were as big as takeout soda lids, and the vein in her neck stuck out. Did I look as scared as she did?

I crept toward the front window.

Billie tripped and pulled the back of my T-shirt, the neck choking me.

"Billie!" I whispered loudly.

She let go and picked up her flip-flop.

"It broke," she whispered. She tried to put it back on, but it dangled from her foot like bait.

"Forget it," I whispered, keeping an eye out for Shiny Head. "You'll just have to hold it. Maybe we can fix it."

Billie gave me a desperate look. She was going to cry again, or worse, throw up.

"Come on. Let's look out the window and see if Dad's outside."

She took a deep breath and nodded as she tried to jam the flip-flop into her shorts pocket. It stuck out awkwardly, slapping her on the side when she walked.

We hunched down behind the cash register and listened. Under the counter there were stacks of papers, a broken coffee mug, and about a million empty packs of cigarettes. I pushed the cartons away and spied an old black telephone.

A telephone!

Yes! I could call Julie.

I pointed silently to the phone and motioned talking on it to Billie. Could I remember Julie's phone number by heart? It was written down in my notebook, but I had to try. I reached for the phone.

Suddenly, we heard voices outside. I spit on the edge of my T-shirt and rubbed dirt off the corner of the window.

"What's wrong?" asked Billie.

I shook my head and peered through the window blinds. It took a minute for my eyes to adjust to the brightness outside, but then I saw him.

Shiny Head was talking to some guy in a cowboy hat. The man was tall, a lot taller than Shiny Head. He had on blue jeans, cowboy boots, and a plaid shirt. His face was hard and mean, like those hunters on the Discovery Channel. The blue car still sat in the parking lot. The Lavender Lady was messing with something in her trunk.

The cowboy kept nodding his head. But I couldn't hear what they were saying.

Was it the sheriff Shiny Head said he called? I made a list in my head:

1. No uniform.
2. No polished badge.
3. No police car.

Conclusion: It wasn't the sheriff.

Shiny Head's crooked back was toward me, but just by watching him I could see he had a lot to say. He kept moving his hands. His arms went up and down, up and down, like he might fly away. Then he pointed toward the gas station, and I knew he was talking about us. They both turned and looked right at me.

Break it up!

Billie pulled on my shirt. "What?" she whispered. "What do you see? Is it Dad?"

I grabbed her hand and dragged her back toward the bathroom. I scanned the gas station, looking for another exit.

"Remember what I said about running?"

She nodded. "But my shoe's broken."

Then I saw it. Near the bathroom, behind a pile of boxes, there was a back door with the words *EMERGENCY EXIT* scrawled across the top in black marker. I leaned against the boxes and pushed. They were heavy.

"I know. You're going to have to forget about your flip-flop. You're a cheetah, Billie. Run as fast as a cheetah. Come on, help me."

Billie pushed with her scrawny arms. Any minute, I expected Shiny Head to burst through the front door, jangling the bells that hung on the doorknob. But all I could hear was the blood rushing through my ears.

Finally, the boxes budged. Clenching my eyes shut, I pushed with every bit of strength I had. I thought about the lady I saw on TV who moved a car just to save her kid. That was me. I had super strength. I did.

And then the boxes moved some more, just enough room for Billie and me to squeeze through. I tried the door handle and it wasn't locked.

"Remember our plan. Run like the prairie dogs."

Billie nodded. And then I saw that frozen deer look.

"You can do it," I said. "Run fast."

I pulled the door open a crack.

Then I heard the bells on the front door jangle. Boots stomped across the floor. My heart jumped, bumped, and banged, but I would not let it panic. Billie would never see me do that.

Fight or flight.

I wedged myself between the door and the boxes and pushed her outside.

"Run! Run! Don't look back!" I yelled.

The break up had begun. We had to break it up so we could stay together.

Billie's hair flew behind her. Her bare foot slapped the

pavement as she ran toward the burned-out car sitting in the desert brush. She was halfway there.

"Hey!"

I spun around. It was Shiny Head pointing a skinny finger right at me, and like a mountain, Cowboy stood behind him.

I tried to pull the door open a little more, but the boxes still sat like boulders blocking my way. I hoped I was as skinny as Billie. Shiny Head rushed toward me, hand outstretched like a claw. I ducked my head through the door.

Freedom!

But my body stuck.

The door pressed hard against my rib cage, and my back wedged against the frame. Billie was skinnier than me. Someone grabbed the back of my shirt. Adrenaline shot through my body.

Fight or flight.

I pushed with all my strength, and the boxes finally shifted. I squeezed through the door and felt my T-shirt rip as I pulled loose. I ran as if my life depended on it. And it did. Billie and me were like endangered species.

Before I left the asphalt, I took one last look at the gas station and saw a hand reach through the slightly open door.

Running as fast as I could, I went in the exact opposite direction as Billie. My heart felt like it was connected to her on a string. The farther away I ran, the tighter it pulled, until I felt all cinched up.

She slipped behind a boulder.

I had to lead Shiny Head and Cowboy away from her. I ran toward a little hill and ducked into the brush.

Stay away. Stay away.

I hoped they wouldn't find her. I hoped they wouldn't find me. Were the prairie dogs as scared as me while they waited for the snake to come? Did they feel any better once they had escaped?

So why didn't I?

Survival Strategy #7:
CAMOUFLAGE

CRAWLING ON MY HANDS AND KNEES, I inched my way to where I thought Billie was hidden. Behind me, Cowboy and Shiny Head stomped around in the desert brush, calling for us.

"Hey, girls!" said Shiny Head. "Come on out. We're not going to hurt you."

Not even for a second did I believe that. Maybe it was the way his voice crept up my spine and stayed there. Pebbles and stones cut into my hands and knees. Before I came here, I thought desert sand was like beach sand, but it wasn't. It's hard and dry and rocky. Nothing at all like the beach. Dry brush scratched my face, and my dirty T-shirt blended in perfectly with the weeds that were as high as my body. Camouflaged.

Camouflage is the most important part of desert survival . . . besides venom. If you have venom you're, like, invincible. In my opinion the top three strategies for desert survival are:

1. Venom.
2. Camouflage.
3. Speed.

If you're a poisonous snake or a scorpion, you're okay. But I wasn't a snake or a scorpion. So I had to rely on three things:

1. Camouflage.
2. Brains.
3. Sound.

And my ears told me that Shiny Head and Cowboy were getting closer.

"Come out and talk to us," said Cowboy. He kicked the bushes in front of him. They were at least two semitruck-lengths away and too close to where Billie was supposed to be hidden.

I willed her to stay with my mind control.

Stay. Stay. Stay.

Mom told me about dangerous people who wanted to

hurt kids. They'd act real nice. And then, forget it—
sometimes they'd keep you forever, or worse. I wouldn't
be fooled that easily.

Thorns poked through my jeans and tiny rocks stuck
into my palms, but I ignored them. Sometimes survival
meant pain. Squatting deeper into the brush, I watched
Shiny Head and Cowboy like a cheetah watches her
prey.

Cowboy stopped and looked back toward the gas
station. "Didn't you say there were three girls?" he
called.

Shiny Head shook his head. "Two." He was only a few
feet from Billie.

I stood up and sucked in my breath. I had to do something. "Hey—" But my words were swallowed up by
Shiny Head, who tripped on something and fell to the
ground.

He rolled around, cursing and moaning.

"Little white trash nothings!" he yelled.

I crouched back down to watch.

"I think I broke my ankle," said Shiny Head.

Cowboy pulled him up.

Shiny Head limped toward the gas station. "Stupid
kids."

"Let's go on back," Cowboy said. "I need to radio
Chuck."

Radio Chuck? He turned and glared out at the desert. Then he and Shiny Head went back into the gas station.

I couldn't trust anyone. No way was I going to let them get us.

Survival Strategy #8:
ESCAPE, IF YOU DARE

"BILLIE," I WHISPERED. *"BILLIE."* BEHIND
the boulder, where she should have been, I found nothing but a Twinkie wrapper licked clean.

Scrambling, I searched everywhere around the boulder, but she had disappeared.

Suddenly, I spied a long brown shape. Was it a snake?
No, just a stick. But it reminded me of something very
important Dad told me. When walking through the desert, you should always make noise to scare away predators, like:

1. Talking.
2. Singing.
3. Shuffling your feet.

But right now I didn't care about any of that. Let the rattlesnakes come. I ran toward the back of the gas station, scanning the brush for a flash of Billie's hair. I whispered her name again, but there was nothing but dirt and red ants.

I rounded the corner, and there she was, crying behind the ice machine.

"Billie," I said, pulling her into a bear hug. "What are you doing? I told you to stay behind the boulder."

She nodded. "I thought you left. I couldn't see you. I thought you left with that man in the cowboy hat."

"I would never leave you. Never."

"Here," said Billie, pulling away. She handed me my notebook.

"Where was it?" I asked, clasping it to my chest.

"In the dirt."

Water flooded my eyes, but I blinked it back. "Come on," I said, grabbing Billie's arm. I wasn't going to lose her again.

Shiny Head and Cowboy were nowhere to be seen. The blue car still sat, but where was the Lavender Lady? What was taking her so long?

Billie and me hunched down and crept closer. I tried to peer inside the back window of the blue car, but the backseat looked like someone's closet. Clothes hung in a long straight row along a bar stretched across the inside of the car, completely covering the back window. A shrunken someone sat in the driver's seat, but it wasn't the Lavender Lady.

I inched Billie and me toward the empty highway, not knowing what else to do. We obviously couldn't stay here. I hesitated and turned back toward the gas station.

"Where are we going?" asked Billie.

Suddenly the gas station door opened and the Lavender Lady slid toward her car.

"Billie," I said, pulling her with me. "Follow me. And be *silent*."

Billie nodded.

I crept to the opposite side of the blue car as the Lavender Lady. Blood whooshed through my veins, and it felt like my heart might pop. But that didn't matter, because when she opened her door, I opened the back door on the opposite side. It clicked open easily. I pushed Billie in, swishing her through dry cleaner bags and long gauzy dresses. I slid in after her, swimming in a cocoon of plastic and fabric. Silently I pulled the door closed. Billie and me crouched behind the seats, surrounded in a perfect, hidden nest.

"Orson!" said the Lavender Lady, still standing outside the car.

I grabbed Billie's hand and squeezed. *Please don't make a sound.* But I didn't even need to try to use my mind powers, because she knew. The look on her face said it all—she would not make a peep.

"What do you think you're doing?" The Lavender Lady demanded. "Orson, no driving for you. I know you think you're well enough, but honest to God, you will kill us."

Orson mumbled something.

"Nope. Nope. Get out." She shoved her BeDazzled bag through the rack of clothes and into the back. It sat perched on the hump in the middle of the floor like it was watching us, right under Billie's nose.

"Let me drive. Orson, I said *out*!"

I gulped and peeked out the back window. Cowboy was standing there. Staring at the blue car like he had laser beams for eyes. Like he could see us crouched in sweat and plastic and cloth.

I ducked and pulled Billie down with me.

Now I had to use my ears. That's what animals do when they're trapped. They use all their senses. Every one. And I wasn't going to be caught lacking now. I closed my eyes and listened.

The Lavender Lady made shuffling noises, and then it was quiet for a second. Then she was on the other side of the car with Orson.

"Come on," she grunted, like she was carrying something heavy. "I've gotcha."

A deep voice murmured something.

"I don't know where your cane is right now. Use your legs and lean on me. *Lean on me.*"

Then, I think Orson got into the seat in front of me. And the Lavender Lady got into the seat in front of Billie.

"There!" she exclaimed. "That's better."

Orson mumbled.

"You would not believe the filth inside that place! And I had to wait forever for that dingbat attendant to ring me up. I sat and waited and waited. I have half a mind to call the owner," said the Lavender Lady. The sound of her voice was ten times the normal talking voice. Orson obviously couldn't hear very well. Hooray for deafness.

The engine clicked and then purred. Even through our cocoon, a blast of cool air shot toward the backseat.

Orson grunted and said something, but I couldn't understand a word. Plastic crinkled.

"No, they didn't have the ones you like. That was all I could find. *That's all they had,*" she said louder. "Old broke-down gas station out in the middle of nowhere. I was lucky they had anything we wanted. Broke-down, just like us, huh, Orson?"

Orson mumbled.

"Never mind," she said. *"I said never mind."*

The car pulled forward slowly. The more it inched toward the road, the more the knots surrounding my heart loosened. We were doing it! I could almost breathe. I didn't care where we were going, or in what direction. All I knew was that we needed to get away from the Jiffy Co. Gas Station and predators like Cowboy and Shiny Head.

From my window, I saw the gas pumps roll past. The road should only be just a few feet away. Would we actually make it? Then the car jerked and the Lavender Lady slammed on her brakes.

"Well, I never!" she exclaimed.

Survival Strategy #9:
TIMING IS EVERYTHING

MY HEART STOPPED. LIKE SOMEONE HAD plunged it into a bucket full of cold water. Was this what it felt like to have a heart attack? I had always wondered. Some animals have one the moment before they are devoured.

Billie grabbed my hand. Her eyes were afraid, but trusting.

I heard the car window roll down.

"Can I help you, officer?" The Lavender Lady sounded annoyed.

Cowboy's voice rumbled through the open window and filled the car.

"Yes. Yes, you can," he said. "I'm Sheriff Boyce. We're

looking for two little girls who were here. We think they may have been abandoned."

Immediately I hated that word: *abandoned*. Like we had no one in the universe who could care for us. Didn't he know I was in charge?

"Oh, dear," said the Lavender Lady. "Those poor things."

"Um, yes. Yes they are," said Cowboy. He sounded like he had a mouth full of rocks. And at least now I knew he was a real sheriff. All the more reason to steer clear of him.

"Have you seen any girls on their own or maybe even with someone? About yea tall?" he asked.

The Lavender Lady must have shaken her head.

"Have you seen anything suspicious at all?" he asked.

Orson mumbled something.

"What did he say?" asked Cowboy.

Yes, what did Orson say? Had he seen us? He seemed so frail and useless, I hadn't really worried too much about him knowing we were here, but now worry bubbled through my blood like carbonation. Should we run for it?

I slipped my hand through the backseat door handle.

"Oh, don't mind my little brother," the Lavender Lady said. "He had a stroke a few years back that affected his speech, but he's as sharp as a tack. We're on our way back from visiting my granddaughter. I hardly ever get to see her, and she just had a baby, so I said to myself, why not? It's been quite a drive, and we're just on our way home—"

Cowboy interrupted. "We're really anxious to find these girls. It's hot out and we have to make sure they're safe."

I inched the handle open, felt it resist as I pulled it toward me, on the verge of a click, which would release us into the heat where we could run and run.

Orson mumbled something again.

"He said he hasn't seen anything."

"Okay then," said Cowboy, thumping the hood. "Thanks for your help. Here's my card in case you think of anything."

"Sure thing," said the Lavender Lady.

The window rolled up. The car pulled forward. And Billie, me, Orson, and the Lavender Lady drove away into a long stretch of road that held only one hope for Billie and me: to call Julie at our next stop. But it drove us away from Cowboy, Shiny Head, and even Dad . . . who if he had wanted to come back and claim us couldn't now, because we were gone. There was something sweet in that.

Suddenly, I felt better. I was in control, even if it meant being chauffeured into who-knew-where by a loud-talking old lady bedecked in lavender and her deaf baby brother.

The floor of the car hummed as the wheels plowed down the highway; the heat from the road warmed the carpet where we sat. I stretched out onto the floor with Billie and linked her hand through mine. I didn't know what was going to happen when the car stopped, but right now I didn't care. We were safe for the moment. I closed my eyes and tried to relax.

I could relax now, couldn't I? Even if it was just for a minute.

Survival Strategy #10:
BEWARE OF TRAPS

AT THE BEGINNING OF THE SUMMER, TWO weeks after Mom died, we got into Dad's camper and drove away—thinking he would make everything better. Dad was finally back. But it was like having to trade one parent for another.

A trap.

I thought being with him would be like magic, everything I had ever imagined. But that was a trap, too.

After we put Mom in the ocean, a week later Dad came and got us. He picked us up at Julie's condo, across from ours. Julie thought Dad was probably going to sell our condo, which sounded pretty awful because what about my best friend, Antonio, who lived next door and who had a real, live tarantula *and* a bearded dragon? And when school started I was supposed to go on the seventh grade overnight trip to Catalina Island, which was crawling with wild boar (I really wanted to see a wild boar up close). And could we take our goldfish, George and Martha? When we got them, Mom said Billie and me would kill them in a week, but I had been very responsible about feeding them and changing their water just right, and so far they had lasted over a year.

What would happen to them?

But then I thought about it some more. If Dad sold our condo, then that probably meant we would get to travel with him everywhere he went, like Puerto Rico, and China, and the Amazon rain forest (although I wasn't very excited about the rain forest because I read in school that the Amazonian people were hunters and gatherers and sometimes ate wild monkey or alligator, and I didn't want to eat that; but I did like granola bars, and trail mix, and fruit rolls, so I could probably just eat those). I bet Dad had already planned it all out for us and it would be okay, because I would do anything to be with him again.

Billie and me had already packed our bag. Julie had the key to our condo and promised to lock it up tight and to take care of George and Martha because this summer we would be living with Dad in his camper. And I was so excited/scared that I could have thrown up the chocolate chip pancakes that Julie had made for us that morning.

Before Mom died, I didn't know Julie could cook more than takeout, because if she came over for girls' night, that's all she ever brought.

The doorbell rang. Julie opened the door and smiled a huge smile like she saw someone she could hardly wait to see.

Dad stepped inside.

"Sam?" said Julie in a high voice. "How are you?"

Dad, taller than I'd thought he'd be, still had his back to us. He let Julie shake his hand. "Hi," he said in a voice I wasn't sure if I remembered.

I held my breath. He was really here.

"And the girls," said Julie, spinning him toward us. "Liberty and Billie. Of course you remember them."

Dad nodded.

Did he?

"Would you like a Coffee Crisp or anything?" Julie asked, walking over to her jars of candy.

Dad shook his head. "I'm fine."

The last time I'd seen Dad, I was six and Billie was two. Mom said he met us at McDonald's (because it had a PlayPlace). I always had questions about the Last Time We Saw Dad, like if I heard the story enough I might find a clue to explain why he never came back. But Mom didn't like to talk about that.

I remembered how Billie screamed in her high chair

and I unbuckled her to let her get on the big slide. Also, Dad ate two Big Macs, which seemed like a lot of Big Macs compared to the four Chicken McNuggets that Billie and me shared.

Mom said when he came in he needed a shower and he hadn't slept in days. He said he had been camping. I didn't remember that part. But I remembered the crying part. When Mom cried after Dad left. She said Billie got stuck at the top of the indoor slide and Mom sent me to get her out, but Billie wouldn't come. That part I remembered, because I was scared to climb all the way up, and I wanted to stay by Dad, and the slide smelled like dirty diapers and French fries.

And then Dad climbed up, his long legs folding onto the slide like a praying mantis. And he grabbed Billie kind of rough, probably because she was kicking and screaming, and he brought her down the slide. He carried her away from his body and gave her to Mom.

Mom said the last thing he said was, "Here."

And then he walked out.

I didn't remember that, but I did have a memory of him waving at me through Ronald McDonald's face painted on the restaurant window. After that Mom said she didn't know where he was for a year and a half, and that's when she got a divorce, and there was nothing he could do about it because he had disappeared. She said he was an unreliable genius and not good around people.

After a while Mom said she saw his pictures in a magazine, so she knew he wasn't dead. But he might as well have been, because after that he only ever sent me one thing in my entire life.

In Julie's condo, Dad smiled at us. He didn't look like a genius, or unreliable, or not good around people. Actually, he looked a lot like Billie. Or Billie looked like Dad. And I already knew that from the pictures I saw of him. But looking at him, standing right in front of me, he really looked like Billie. He even had invisible white eyebrows like hers.

"You've gotten big," he said to Billie. He picked her up like she was a baby. And I thought she'd get mad, but she didn't say anything. Dad said, "The last time I saw you, you were just a baby."

"I know," whispered Billie.

"I have something for you," he said, still looking at Billie. He dug around in his backpack and pulled out a little stuffed koala bear. "It's from Australia."

Billie smiled shyly and hugged it. I already knew Dad had been to Australia because once, when I was Billie's age, I saw some pictures he took in a magazine when he was there.

Finally he looked at me. "Hi, Liberty." He reached out

awkwardly and grabbed my hand. His was rough and scratchy. "I brought you this." He pulled something out of his bag. "But I think you might be too old for it now."

It was a bug hut. You know, the kits you get when you're about five years old to collect spiders and stuff? I used to have one. I used to really love it.

"When you were little, you were crazy about catching bugs," he said.

"Thanks." It was nice of him to bring me something, even if I was too old for it.

And that's when I remember being really mad at Mom. How long had she kept him from us? He seemed nice, just sort of shy.

Dad came in and sat on Julie's couch while Billie and me played Go Fish out on the balcony. He crossed his legs and swung his foot as Julie talked and talked and talked.

He and Julie talked for a long time, and most of it I couldn't hear, until Julie finally stood up and walked toward the door to the deck.

She said, "It sounds like you've been doing really well. I'm happy to hear it. I have a good feeling about this. The girls are so excited. Where are you guys headed?"

"We're going to scout out some locations in the desert."

"All summer?" asked Julie.

"Yep," said Dad.

"Living in your camper?" she asked, her eyes wide.

"Yep," Dad said. "They'll love it."

We would, right? Dad was finally back. I'd make sure that Billie and me loved it.

Survival Strategy #11:
SOMETIMES YOU SHOULD FEEL SORRY FOR THE COBRA

JULIE CAME AND GOT US FROM THE DECK. "Are you excited?"

I nodded and squeezed Billie's hand.

"If you need me, you can call. You have my phone numbers, right? Home and cell?"

I nodded. I had them written in my notebook.

She pulled on her watch that was a bracelet, too. "I'm just going to be working all summer. So you call about anything, okay?"

"Yes," I said.

She handed Dad a piece of paper with her phone numbers written on it. "Call me with any questions," she said. "But you don't have to worry; they're good girls."

Dad nodded.

"It will be fine." She patted my arm.

But we wouldn't need to call her. Why would we? We had our dad now.

She steered me toward him and put her arm around Billie, smiling too big. "You guys are really going to love getting acquainted after all these years."

Billie smiled at Dad. I thought she liked him already. Maybe I did, too.

Dad looked sort of embarrassed. And maybe scared, like Antonio's bearded dragon when I reached into his cage to pick him up. Spike got all squirmy, kicking dust all over the place. Antonio said it was because he wasn't comfortable with me yet. Maybe new/old dads and bearded dragons were the same.

Julie said to Dad, "Children really do belong with family after such tragedies. Don't you agree, Sam? You're ready for it, right? I mean, you feel good about it?"

Dad nodded.

She looked around her living room, running her hands through her hair. "My house is quite small for two girls."

And really, it was. Her condo had two bedrooms like

ours, but the extra bedroom was her office. At first Billie and me had wanted to stay in our own feels-like-Mom condo, and she let us for the first few nights. But then Julie got tired of sleeping on our sofa, since she wouldn't sleep in Mom's room, and she said that we had to stay with her. Her condo was so close, we could just run home to get whatever we needed. We slept in the office on the pullout sofa.

I figured after our summer with Dad things would be more official and if we didn't go to the Amazon or China, maybe Dad wouldn't sell our condo. Maybe we could stay and he could take pictures of things in San Diego. When I told Antonio that, he said I was loco. He said that my mom told his mom that Dad was a loner. He said that my mom told his mom that Dad was a deadbeat. What did Antonio's mom know, anyway?

Mom said Antonio's mom was a busybody. Mom didn't care about gossip; she was too worried about taking care of us. Plus, having kids was really expensive, so Mom had to work a lot. Mom said that all the time. And that's why if I ever got a birthday invitation, I didn't even show it to her because we didn't have money to waste on a present. And really, who cared about that when I knew my invitation was only because we were in the same class at school? When I saw Mom working herself into a sand-crab ball, scrunched up onto the couch, so tired from three night shifts in a row, then I felt bad. I always tried hard to not be expensive.

Anyway, what did Antonio know about anything? He ate dinner with his nosy mom and his dad and his brother every night—he didn't know about missing dads. But the one good thing about Antonio's mom was that she let me come over and hold Spike even if Antonio was at soccer practice. And usually she had extra tamales, or empanadas, or a Coke for me. Antonio's mom was a good cook.

Usually Antonio was a decent friend. He liked animals, he lived close, and he didn't always have to be talking. Being friends with him was better than having to be friends with Suzanne and the girls from my sixth grade class. All their talking and giggling and their liking-of-boys made me tired. Antonio was easy even if he wasn't always nice. I just ignored the bad parts of him. Sometimes you have to do that with people.

Julie turned away from Dad and shoved a Snickers bar into my hand. "It's going to be fine. And if it's not, you call." She had chocolate on her front tooth.

"Okay," I whispered.

Then I pulled Billie closer to me and squeezed her hand. I'd make sure everything would be perfect. I'd do it because I had to.

We loaded our suitcase into the camper—Billie and me shared Mom's big one. Then Dad showed us around.

The camper was old, but it had a little fridge and a little shower and a big bed for Dad and a smaller one for Billie that folded right out of the cabinet above the kitchen table. And I would sleep on a bed that you could make out of couch cushions and the kitchen table. It was pretty smart. Maybe this living in a camper would be fun.

That first day, Dad let us sit up front with him on the long bench, with seat belts that had fallen behind us like snake tongues. And Billie sat by Dad. And I sat by the window. We drove the longest I had ever driven in a car. Hours and hours. Dad said we were still in California, but I didn't believe him until he showed me the map. California was *big*—filled with freeways and deserts and roads where you could drive for hours and still be in the same state. Soon, Julie was gone. And so was San Diego. And so was the ocean, with Mom in it.

That day Dad didn't talk a whole lot. But he tried, at first. "You look like your mom."

"I know," I said. Because I did know. Everyone said that.

"Your hair is the same color. And you have her forehead."

I nodded. Same brown hair. Same big forehead.

He cleared his throat. "So, you doing okay? After everything . . ."

I shrugged. "Yeah."

"I'm really sorry about Cindy," he said. Cindy was my mom's name.

"Yeah, I know," I said. I felt uncomfortable talking about Mom, especially to him. "But we're glad you're here now."

Billie smiled to herself and hugged her koala.

Dad smiled, too.

There was a whole part of me that didn't even believe Mom was dead yet. Or that this dad I had always hoped for was sitting next to me. Did he make chocolate chip pancakes? Was he going to tell us everything he knew about animals? Did he have a notebook just like me?

Having Dad back was supposed to be like magic. Everything should feel normal, right? But it was just weird. I held on to my notebook because it was the only thing that felt real.

"What is that?" he asked.

"My notebook," I said, flattening it onto my lap. It felt safer there. "Just stuff I write. About animals and things I like."

Dad coughed. "You're interested in animals?"

I nodded.

Billie stared.

"Nice," said Dad.

But that's all he said. And I wanted to ask him

questions, but they stuck in my throat like that time I had a fever and Mom gave me three Advil to swallow. The questions stuck and wouldn't come out.

Finally, after an hour or so, the silence began to bother me. Shouldn't we be able to talk to him like we had talked to Mom? He was ours now, wasn't he?

I swallowed hard and said, "So, where have you been?"

He cleared his throat and scrunched his lips together. "I've been working." He sounded a little irritated.

I rubbed an imaginary spot off the dashboard. "Oh. Do you like being a photographer?"

"Yes."

"Where do you live?"

"All over."

"What do you like to take pictures of?"

"Everything."

And then I pulled out a clipping from my notebook. It was a picture of a king cobra from the *Kids Discover* magazine subscription Dad had sent us about two years after he left. As far as I knew, it was the only thing he had ever sent Billie or me. "I really like this picture."

And he said, "I can't believe you still have that."

Then he told me all about getting that shot in India. And how it would have been easier to go to a snake charmer to get the picture, but he wanted the snake to be a healthy cobra, not one that had had its mouth sewn shut. So instead, he took a picture of a cobra in the wild.

"Why do they sew their mouths shut?" I asked, not believing that snake charmers would really do that.

"So they won't get bitten."

"But then how does the cobra eat?" I asked.

"It can't," Dad said. "Eventually it dies."

The older I got, the more I realized people did all sorts of stupid things, just because they could.

"That's sad," Billie whisper-said, squeezing her koala bear tight.

Dad nodded. "Cobra venom is lethal. But in my experience, cobras aren't as scary as they seem. You just have to know how to behave around them."

I thought maybe that was true about missing dads, too.

That was my best day with Dad, by far. Maybe it was the adventure of it. Or the summer days stretched out before us. Or maybe I finally realized how much I missed having a dad. That day, bumping down the desert road with him beside me talking about cobras and smelling like a campfire, I realized I had missed him a whole lot more than I had ever imagined.

But that was a trap, and the worst part was, I didn't even know it.

Survival Strategy #12:
NEST AND REST

NOW, ON THE HIGHWAY WITH THE LAVENDER
Lady and Orson, the darkness cradled me like a baby
bird tucked into a nest of blackness, turning me and Billie into downy balls covered in feathers and sticks and
dryer lint. Anyway, that's what most nests are made out
of. You couldn't even tell it was us. *Poof.* We had disappeared like magic. No one on the entire planet knew we
were here. It felt good to be invisible—invincible—in
the dark.

Did you know most nocturnal animals live in the
desert? I always preferred nocturnal animals anyway,
like owls, and hamsters, and mice. Mice really are the cut-
est things. And so smart. But Billie had always wanted
a cat.

I stretched my foot farther under Orson's seat, hoping he couldn't feel it. The hairs inside my ears perked up. Orson snored, and the Lavender Lady hummed to the radio. Outside, the sky was dark. How long had we been driving? My watch said 7:57. Six hours. Billie's hair splayed across my hand and became tangled in between my fingers. The rest of her was scrunched up into a little nest-ball near the door. I felt around the floor of the car for my tennis shoes.

The snoring stopped. Then it started again. Orson coughed so loud, it made me jump, and Billie, too. But she did it in her sleep and didn't even notice. Reflexes always work, even in your dreams.

The tires bumped over the highway and slowed to a stop. The car turned to the right. And then the left. Then it jerked and stopped again, like maybe we had hit something.

"Where did that curb come from?" asked the Lavender Lady. She opened her door.

Orson woke up, grumbling like a California grizzly.

"No. Not yet," she said. "We're just stopping here for the night. Five more hours tomorrow. I'll check us in. No. *No. Just stay.*" The door slammed.

The rustling in Orson's seat stopped.

Billie sat up and rubbed her eyes. "Where are—"

I covered her mouth. *Shh.* I pointed to where Orson

70

sat, but he didn't move. I needed to use the bathroom, and I'm sure Billie did, too. Orson shifted in his seat. Then an old, gnarled hand poked through the curtain of clothes, almost brushing against my forehead. Billie and me shrank back.

The front door swung open again. "I forgot my purse." Now the Lavender Lady's hand joined Orson's, swinging dangerously near us through the clothes. "Stop it, Orson. I've got it. Sit back. *Orson, I've got it!*"

Billie grabbed the purse and shoved it into the Lavender Lady's hand.

"There it is," she exclaimed. "I swear I'd lose my head if it wasn't attached." She slammed the door again and walked away.

I stared at Billie. Usually she never did stuff like that. She was only brave around people she knew.

She shrugged. *What?*

I made a tunnel through the clothes and peeked at Orson. He was unconscious again.

Billie whispered, "I need to go to the bathroom."

I nodded. "So do I. Let's just wait until she gets back."

Billie made a face. "I need to go now."

I looked around the backseat. There was nothing, just some clothes and garment bags. Should she pee on the floor? But I couldn't let her. Animals don't sleep where they pee. And the Lavender Lady, even though she didn't know it, was doing us a huge favor—we couldn't pee in her car.

But now the spell was broken. Reality was setting in. We'd have to leave our nest eventually, wouldn't we? We had to call Julie. We couldn't just ride with the Lavender Lady to her house and yell, *Surprise!*

I had to find a phone.

I poked my head up and peered out the window. We were parked at a hotel. The parking lot was nearly empty. I hesitated. Billie was jiggling her knee and holding herself.

"Liberty!" Billie whispered.

"I know."

I stole a sideways look at Orson. He had a jowly face that was covered in wrinkles, like a pug. Pug dogs were pretty cute, even though they weren't nocturnal creatures. His eyes were closed and squished into their sockets. His hearing aid had fallen out of his ear and grazed his shoulder. I listened more closely. His snoring stopped. His chest sat unmoving. Was he breathing?

I inched my face a little closer. He smelled like a fat, buttery pretzel, like the ones you buy at the mall.

Billie pulled on the back of my shirt.

I waved her away. Was he dead? A minute passed on the car clock. It said 8:05.

Breathe.

I had to do something.

The belly under his plaid shirt stayed still. It creeped me out to think we were trapped in a car with someone who had just died, even if he did smell like something good to eat. I lifted my hand and, without thinking, reached out and poked him in the chest.

He sat up and began coughing. The car rocked with each hacking cough, and something rattled in his lungs. It sounded awful.

I ducked behind the rod of clothes and pulled Billie down with me.

The coughing continued, and Billie whispered, "What did you do?"

I shook my head. "Nothing."

She grimaced and pointed at a wet spot on the carpet. "What? Why . . ."

"He scared it out of me," she said, scooching out of the puddle and coming over onto my side. It already smelled like pee in the backseat. We had to get out of here. But I could hear the *tap-tap-tap* of the Lavender Lady's shoes coming closer.

It was time to do something.

Survival Strategy #13:
TAKE IT

THE CAR DOOR OPENED.

"That's all settled. We're room two-oh-two," the Lavender Lady said, tossing her purse back through the rack of clothes so it perched on top of Billie's stomach. She sat on top of me, her wet shorts seeping into mine.

I shoved her over, our butts wedged next to each other on the floor. The clothes in plastic swirled around us. It was getting hot. I shoved the purse over into the wet spot, but then I stopped. I wrapped my fingers around the handle.

Orson continued to cough.

"What got you so up in arms?" asked the Lavender Lady. I heard rustling from the front of the car. "Here's your water," she said. *"Orson. Water."*

I heard gulping, and then the coughing stopped. She turned on the engine and slowly drove through the parking lot. I pulled the purse closer.

Billie looked at me, questions in her eyes.

My heart bumped.

The smell of pee was stronger now—it filled my nose and hair and eyes. I blinked back the burn. The Lavender Lady would notice any second. But still, I could not let go of the purse.

Billie's stomach let out a gurgle.

Mom had always said, "Billie does whatever you do. You are the example." I knew that. Did she think I didn't know that?

Billie pushed the hair out of her eyes and shook her head back and forth, just a little. I guess her mind powers were working.

A tingle ran up my back. I ignored it. What else could I do? The Lavender Lady was practically begging me to open her purse. How long had we sat back here with it? Billie and me, we had nothing.

Somehow I knew that if I could talk to the Lavender Lady, really look into her eyes and tell her what had happened to us, she'd help in an instant. Give us every cent she had. Take us to California to find Julie. I stared at the black leather of the seat in front of Billie like I had X-ray eyes. Like I was telling her everything and she listened like there wasn't anyone else in the world. She might even adopt us. I was sure she would. Just like that tiger I saw on the news that adopted piglets, four of them. They put little tiger-print sweaters on them and the tiger fed them and kept them warm, just like their real mom would have done if she had been alive.

But Billie and I were not piglets.

I stared at where we sat curled in plastic and pee and thought maybe we were, just a little. The thought of really asking the Lavender Lady for help made me want to throw up. I couldn't *really* trust her. Usually how people seemed and what they actually did were opposites. Look at what had happened this morning with Dad. What if the Lavender Lady was mad about Billie and me sneaking into her car and about Billie peeing all over it? For sure she would be angry about the pee. There was no way I would ask her for help. Not for real.

The Lavender Lady hummed as the car bumped into a parking spot.

"Okay, Orson, the map says we're in building C. I'm going in first to open our room door and turn on the lights, and then I'll come back and help you."

Orson mumbled.

"I'll be right back."

This was my chance. I grabbed her lavender studded purse and unzipped it—fast. Faster than I thought I could, and then I dumped everything onto the car floor. Receipts, hand sanitizer, some kind of medicine, tissues, her wallet(!), old lady lipstick, some breath mints, and that crumpled-up business card Cowboy had given her.

Billie hunched over me and poked at the tin of breath mints with her skinny finger.

I handed them to her.

She flipped the lid open and dumped them all into her mouth.

While she crunched on those, I unbuttoned the wallet. But then something made me stop. I had never stolen anything in my life, unless you counted the Ring Pop at the grocery store when I was four. (Which I did not, because Mom had marched me back to the store manager to return it and apologize.) But right now I wasn't stealing. I was looking. There was nothing wrong with looking.

Orson started to cough again.

I yanked the wallet open. My heart fluttered, like a hummingbird was trapped inside. Out slipped the Lavender Lady's driver's license. On the top it said CALIFORNIA. She was from California! A straight ride to San Diego . . . maybe. Then: MYRNA ANN HALSTRONG. Born in 1940. Wow, she was really old. I stared at the weird picture with her eyes sort of crossed.

Suddenly, the front door flew open. The voice of Myrna Ann Halstrong, aka the Lavender Lady, rang out.

"That stupid clerk! I swear I told him I wanted a room on the bottom floor." She cursed and slammed the door behind her. "Orson, people don't listen anymore. Nobody listens." She turned the car back on and squealed out of the parking space. "I'm going to give that guy a piece of my mind. I told him there was no way you could climb the stairs." The car jerked forward as she sped back to the front of the hotel to yell at the person who manned the front desk.

Hurry. Hurry.

All I could think of was Billie and me being stranded here with nothing, not even a dollar to make a phone call. I jerked the money out of the wallet and shoved it into my pocket, the bills fat and heavy. Then Billie and I quietly scrambled to put everything back into her bag. Tissues. Lipstick. Sanitizer. I grabbed the empty mint tin under the seat and tossed that in, too. The Lavender Lady still ranted. She parked the car and stomped inside.

Billie chomped on her mints, her cheeks full like the chipmunks we saw at Zion National Park. Now the backseat smelled like pee and breath crystals. I zipped up the bag and set it on the little bump behind the armrest, between the rack of clothes. The money in my pocket poked me in the hip, like an outstretched finger saying *Liberty is a criminal.* Was there such a thing as kid jail?

The lights in the parking lot flicked on. The sun had

78

set and cast shadows across the pavement. The Lavender Lady still yelled at the guy at the desk and Orson fell back to sleep. I stretched up and pulled the money out of my pocket. It was damp with sweat, or maybe Billie's pee.

One. Two. Three. Four twenty-dollar bills sat safely in my hand.

Eighty dollars. How many Twinkies could that buy? No matter how bad I felt about stealing, looking at the wad of money, I knew I would never give it back. Instinct had kicked in.

I turned to Billie. "Come on. Let's get out of here."

Survival Strategy #14:
BEWARE OF "SKIP TO MY LOU"

WHEN BILLIE AND ME MOVED INTO DAD'S camper, I realized he didn't have a TV. Sometimes campers had TVs and stuff, but his didn't. There was a computer, but it was for his work. And I really missed my animal shows. Having a dad was way better than watching any old TV show, though. Still, it was an adjustment. I didn't complain because he had to like us.

After Dad picked us up in San Diego, he said we were headed to Arches National Park in Utah so he could get some pictures of all the rock formations called arches. I was really excited to see them. I had an information pamphlet in my notebook—it was about chipmunks, prairie dogs, tortoises, coyotes, and mule deer who lived there. I had really wanted to see a mule deer.

That first night in the camper we parked at a rest stop and slept inside. The sleeping bag was hot. And for a second, it was so quiet and dark that I felt like maybe we were floating somewhere in outer space. In the middle of the night, Billie fell off her bed and landed right on top of me. So I let her stay next to me, because really her bed was too small and high. When she fell, Dad didn't even wake up. He just slept and slept.

"Tell me a story, Liberty," whispered Billie. Because even though she had a brand-new koala, I could tell she really missed San Diego, and our condo, and George and Martha, and Mom. And maybe so did I, but I didn't want to let Billie know that.

"Once upon a time, there was a sea turtle floating through the ocean all by her lonesome."

Billie nodded.

"And she had a secret. She was going to have baby turtles. But she needed to find a special place where she could hide her eggs so they could grow up happy and strong."

Billie closed her eyes.

"She went to the shore and buried them in the sand . . ."

And just that fast, Billie was asleep again. I could tell by her longish breathing and how her mouth fell open a tiny bit. And for a second I almost woke her back up, because I didn't like feeling alone in the camper. Right then, I missed Mom more, now that we weren't in the condo. My heart felt all dehydrated with the missing of everything: Mom, and our condo, and Antonio, and my school, and even Julie. What could I do to fill it up again?

I climbed up onto Billie's bed and reached around in the covers for the flashlight Dad gave her in case she got scared. It was tucked in between the wall and the mattress. Then I covered myself under Billie's old baby blanket and turned on the light so I could read my notebook with the lists of everything I knew. Sometimes it's the only thing that makes me feel better.

The next morning, in the daylight, I finally saw where we had spent the night: an empty campground surrounded by bushes that looked like long, bony fingers crawling up from the ground.

Sitting outside at the picnic table, Dad pulled out some truck stop cinnamon rolls and apples he had bought yesterday for breakfast. He handed us each an apple. "What's more amazing than a talking llama?" he asked.

Billie and I looked at each other, because how did Dad know we liked jokes?

Finally, Billie said, "I don't know."

"A spelling bee."

Dad laughed. It was a pretty good one.

And Billie said, "What do you call a grizzly bear stuck in the rain?"

"I don't know."

"A drizzly bear."

"That's funny," Dad said. And then he took a huge bite of his apple.

And that missing feeling slowly inched over, leaving space in my heart for something new. And for a second, there in the sun, I felt almost happy.

After we ate our cinnamon rolls, Dad showed us where we could brush our teeth but said we couldn't take a shower inside the camper until we got to a campsite with hookups for water. Then we drove again for hours and hours with nothing to look at but desert. And it was getting sort of boring. And just when I thought I would pop with doing-nothingness, Dad said, "Maybe we should take a detour."

And then we drove through a place called Zion National Park, which was maybe the most beautiful place I had ever seen. I didn't know some mountains were orange like a sunset and could reach so high that it hurt my neck to stare up at them.

Dad stopped for lunch near a stream so we could eat bagels, and he showed us how to skip rocks. Billie was actually really good at it—better than me. My stomach felt heavy when Dad smiled and patted her back after her rock skipped four times before a fish jumped up and swallowed it.

I should be able to skip a rock better than her.

But when I saw Billie's face all golden, I felt guilty. And Mom's words were in my head reminding me, like always, that I was the oldest. That I was supposed to take care of her. And if Billie was happy, then I decided that I could be, too.

"Did you see that, Liberty?" she asked.

I nodded and meant it when I said, "Good job, Billie. You're way better than me."

After that, Dad pulled his camera gear out of the back of the camper and set it on a picnic bench. We sat and watched him go through bags, take out lenses, switch cameras. I didn't know what to do. Were we supposed to go with him? Stay there? He hadn't said.

Billie hugged Koala.

Dad threw his backpack over his shoulder and glanced at the sun and then at us. "Come on. The light is going."

We followed him up the trail.

The cliffs stretched like they scraped the sky. I had to run-walk to keep up with him. Billie had to run-run. She had on her flip-flops and kept tripping. I grabbed her hand to steady her. "I'll go first. Just watch my feet and step where I step," I said.

Pretty soon, Dad started to talk. Out loud. Not really to us; more like to the sky.

He talked about the last time he had been there. How

84

he had almost stepped on a rattlesnake sitting fat and happy, sunning itself in the middle of the trail. And how we should be noisy when hiking so we could give animals time to move out of our way.

Then Dad started whistling "Skip to My Lou."

And I stopped, right there, next to the twisted, gnarled tree that stretched over our path. I stopped because I remembered that whistle. I didn't even know I knew it before. But standing there, listening to my dad, my gone-forever-but-now-he's-back dad, whistle "Skip to My Lou," I knew I had heard it before.

I wondered what else was buried deep inside my brain. What else was going to come up when I didn't even know? What would happen if it all came rushing out?

Survival Strategy #15:
TRUST INSTINCT

SNEAKING OUT OF THE LAVENDER LADY'S car was easier than I thought it would be. I watched her through the glass hotel doors from my hiding spot in the backseat. She banged her fist on the desk like it was a gavel and she was the judge on one of those divorce court shows Mom never liked me to watch. And Orson? Well, you know, he couldn't hear a thing.

The clock said 8:34. I opened the back door and slunk out, Billie right behind me and the money tucked safely in my pocket. I pushed the door closed carefully with a tiny click. We crept past the entrance of the hotel and into the shadows between two bushes. Compared to the car, outside felt cool and refreshing, so much better than sweaty, recycled pee air.

I couldn't hold it any longer. My bladder was going to burst. I pulled my shorts down and crouched. "Don't look," I said.

"Ewwww. That's gross," said Billie when pee hit dried leaves.

I pulled up my shorts. "Not as gross as peeing in your pants."

She looked embarrassed but didn't say anything. There was still a huge wet spot on the back of her shorts. She stepped closer into the bushes, scratching her thighs.

"Stop that," I said.

"I can't help it. Dried pee makes me itch."

We ducked toward the bushes farther away from the parking lot lights and the entrance to the hotel.

Just for a second, I turned around and stared at the car where Orson sat sleeping. Had he stopped breathing again? Did he need someone to poke him back into life? The hotel door creaked open and the Lavender Lady came out, her face transformed into a smile. I had spent so much time sitting behind her; it took me a minute to get used to seeing her from the front. She looked like an old half-bitten apple, baking on the asphalt, all shrunken and wrinkled.

She opened the car door. "Orson, we hit the jackpot. You should see the room upgrade we got. *Orson. Upgrade!*"

The only response she got was Orson's hacking cough again. Good. He was still breathing.

For a minute, I felt sad to leave. But animals on the run don't have time for sadness—they don't feel a thing. I pulled Billie around the corner, ready to face whatever happened next, just the two of us.

Survival Strategy #16:

IF IT'S GOOD ENOUGH FOR A SEA TURTLE, IT MIGHT BE GOOD ENOUGH FOR YOU

DO YOU KNOW HOW A GREEN SEA TURTLE has her babies? She climbs up to shore, digs a hole, lays her eggs, covers them up with sand, and then she goes back to the sea—without *ever* looking back.

The baby turtles are all alone for two whole months, snuggled up, getting warm in the sand and spending their days growing, until they finally hatch. Then they have to hurry back to the water so they can survive. On top of that, they have to watch out for other animals like seagulls and crabs waiting in the dark to eat them. Baby sea turtles don't have their moms to tell them where to go or what to do. But they have *instinct*. Sea turtles just know what to do to survive.

The hotel pool had been easy to find. After Billie and me walked around the building looking for a pay phone, we turned the corner and, *bam*, there it was. Like maybe Mom had sent it down to us from outer space. A perfect place where Billie and me could wash off grime and pee. After that we could find a phone.

Of course, the gate around the pool was locked. The sign said no swimming after nine o'clock, but after taking the Lavender Lady's money, I just kind of decided that the rules didn't apply to Billie and me. I climbed the fence and found a place where Billie could slide through.

Now swimming in the pool, I imagined I was a sea turtle, gliding through the ocean. The moon glistened on my back and my baby sea turtle sister swam next to me. I knew it wasn't true, but it was a nice thought as Billie and I swam naked in the outdoor swimming pool. It was dark, and it was pretty late. No one had walked by, not even once.

The water was still warm from baking in the desert sun all day. I couldn't believe our luck; it was like an oasis just for us. The pool was amoeba-shaped. It had little nooks and crannies, some in very dark spaces, surrounded by hedges and rows of lounge chairs. It felt hidden and safe. But more than anything, it felt good to wash off everything that had happened today.

I wouldn't have believed it if I hadn't just done it. Now I needed to plan our next step. But I couldn't think without making a list. Clasping the edge of the pool to catch my breath, I saw my notebook sitting on the lounge chair I had pulled near a row of hedges. Just seeing it there, waiting for me to fill it with everything I knew, calmed me.

"Liberty, watch." Billie floated on her back in the shallow end. The only light came from the glow of the moon.

"That's awesome," I whispered.

Billie had found an old damp towel that someone had left behind. I spread it out next to a lawn chair, behind a row of bushes. I rinsed Billie's clothes out in chlorine water and laid them on the warm cement to dry.

I swam over to the shadowy side of the pool and pulled myself up. My hands and toes were pruney, and the concrete from the bottom of the pool had chewed away at my feet, leaving the edges raw. I padded over to the towel and wrapped myself up. The breeze tickled my skin and covered me in goose bumps. I glanced up at the hotel floors; there were three levels surrounding the pool, some windows black and some bright like eyeballs, reflecting back the light. Maybe everyone was safe, except for us.

"Billie, come here," I whispered. I didn't have to remind her to be quiet. She knew.

As she swam over, the water rippled behind her like a dolphin tail. The little crease between her eyes deepened, like it had been forever part of her face, a baby S-shaped snake in the center of her forehead. It had crept there and stayed after Mom died.

I knelt down and pulled her closer to me through the water, cocooned in the shadows of the pool.

"I thought of the best joke," I whispered, tucking a strand of hair behind her ear. "What did the baby zebra say to the other baby zebra?"

She balanced a little army man she had found on the ledge. It teetered and fell in. She shook her head. Her flyaway hair had already begun to dry. Her pinched face looked tired.

"No jokes, Liberty. I'm hungry. When are we going to eat?"

I had to face it sometime. Billie never was her best self when she was hungry. I didn't want her to have a meltdown. We needed to find something to eat and we needed to call Julie.

"When's Dad coming? I want Koala."

Dad.

I shoved him out of my brain and locked it tight. I reached for Billie's face so I could get a better look at her cheek. The swelling had gone down, but a purplish bruise had formed.

"Why do you care after he did that to you?" I asked. It should have been me, not her. I had tried to protect her. I really had, but—

"He didn't mean to," Billie said. "It was my fault."

"No, it wasn't."

"Yes, it must have been. Or why would he do it?"

"Because there's something wrong with him," I said.

"Like what?"

I shook my head. I didn't know.

After the first few days, Dad started to change. He forgot what a kid needed. Like a shower, or breakfast, or clothes that didn't smell like sweat or campfires. I had to remind him when we needed to eat. The longer we stayed with Dad, the more he got:

1. Standoffish.
2. Annoyed.
3. Angry.

"It wasn't our fault, Billie. He's the dad. Mom would have never done that to us."

Tears filled her eyes. I shouldn't have said that. Internally, I had banned Mom from our conversations because it made Billie so upset. She let me pull her into an awkward hug. "It's okay. I'm going to take care of us. We're going home."

She pulled away. "We are? Going home! To San Diego? When?" A smile flashed across her face. Her real one. The golden one.

"Yes. We're going home. After tonight, okay? But first I'm going to find a phone."

Billie's voice got whiny. "I'm hungry."

"Shh," I whispered as I helped her out of the water. "Fine. Food first."

I gave her my damp towel and wrapped it around her scrawny little back. I sat her on the lawn chair crouching in the shadows and quickly pulled my clothes over my wet skin.

"Your clothes are still drying, so you sit here in the towel and wait."

She nodded.

I glanced up at the hotel windows; now only three of them had lights on. I squinted, imagining a fly's eye with three thousand lenses staring down, ready to call Cowboy to come and get us.

I tucked Billie farther back onto the chair, deeper into the shadows, hiding my most precious item. The towel was pulled tight around her. Was this how a sea turtle felt after she buried her eggs and slid back into the ocean? Like she might throw up stuff like sea grass and algae that

94

churned in her stomach? Like it was the worst thing she ever had to do, to leave her shiny eggs glittering like gold in the wet sand, where anything might happen to them?

"You stay here and wait for me. I'll be right back."

Billie nodded. She leaned back and closed her eyes. The little crease on her forehead seemed smaller, like maybe she could be almost golden again.

Survival Strategy #17:
ACCLIMATE

THROUGH THE GLASS DOOR, I COULDN'T see anyone at the front desk. I reached into my pocket and touched the money, just to be sure. I leaned in closer. To the right of the front desk there was a little shop inside, but I couldn't tell if it was open. Maybe they had snacks and some flip-flops for Billie.

With Billie alone at the pool I knew I didn't have a lot of time. I pulled the money out of my pocket again and counted it. Yes, eighty dollars. I shoved the guilt and the image of the Lavender Lady's face back into my pocket with the money. What could I do about it now?

A bell echoed through the empty lobby as I opened the door. To the right was the shop. I paused and waited for someone to come out from the door behind the front desk, but nothing happened. All was quiet.

Once, when I was seven, I stayed at a hotel with my mom and Billie when we went to a funeral of my mom's only living relative, her great-aunt. Billie was too little and probably didn't even remember, but I did, especially the elevator.

While Mom was trying to get Billie and our bags inside the elevator, the doors closed. It had gone up a floor with just me inside. At first I screamed Mom's name, but then I stopped because I hated the way my voice echoed against the metal doors. At the top the elevator opened, but no one was there. I curled into the corner and waited and eventually the elevator went back down.

When the door slid open again, Billie said, "Bertie!" (which was the baby way she used to say my name).

And Mom said, "Thank God, Liberty. That's all I need right now—to lose one of you girls." She had shifted Billie onto her other hip. "I knew you'd stay put. You always do the right thing."

She pulled the luggage cart inside and stroked my hair. "What would I ever do without you?"

Little did she know I was the one who would have to do the living without. Even at seven I knew it was my job to be responsible. Always.

Now I inched closer to the shelves stacked with things like tissue and aspirin and Doritos. There were no flip-flops, but there were a few other things to eat mixed in with souvenirs. I crept forward and stood purposely behind the postcard rack, hoping no one would come. The postcards said WELCOME TO WILLIAMS and HELLO FROM THE GRAND CANYON. We were near the Grand Canyon? That was on the way back to California. We had passed the Grand Canyon sign on the way to Four Corners. I had wanted to see it. But Dad said no.

Suddenly, the postcard rack turned and its gears let out a horrible squeal. I jumped back, knocking over a bunch of packages of Nutter Butters that sat behind me. I scrambled to pick them up.

A long dark face with furry caterpillar eyebrows stared down at me. "Can I help you?" he asked as he crouched down to pick up the rest of the cookies.

I stood up. "No. I mean yes. I mean . . ." I tried to stack the Nutter Butter packages, but they kept sliding around like fish skin. I faced Caterpillar Eyebrows and took a deep breath, trying to quiet the spiders in my stomach. "My-mom-sent-me-down-for-some-aspirin-she's-got-a-terrible-headache," I said, and snatched the aspirin off the shelf.

He paused. The caterpillar eyebrows stopped wiggling. *Please believe me.*

He shuffled toward the cash register. "All righty then." He punched a button on the machine and held out his hand. "Is that it?"

We couldn't eat aspirin for dinner. I needed food. I shook my head. *Pull it together, Liberty. Fake it.* It was just like before when we stayed at a hotel with Mom. I could make myself believe that she really was upstairs in bed with a headache. It was true. I willed myself to pretend it was true.

"Uhh. No." I slid back to the shelves, pulling things off, making sure I stayed clear of the Nutter Butters. "I'll take these, too." I set an armful of junk food down on the counter.

He eyed my pile suspiciously.

Now I stared at it, too. Turkey jerky. Sunflower seeds. Potato chips. Mini doughnuts. Mentos. Peanut butter crackers (Billie loved peanut butter crackers). Not really the dinner I was hoping for, but . . . "I'll take these, too." I sat two bottles of water right next to everything else. "My mom hates to take medicine on an empty stomach."

Slowly, he started scanning my items. "Well, I don't know if this is going to set too well with aspirin, but—"

"Do you have anything healthier?"

He shook his head. "Not unless she wants to wait until morning. That's when we do the continental breakfast. But then it's just bagels and oatmeal."

"Oh, the breakfast?"

"Yep, comes free with every night booked. Didn't Doreen tell you that when you checked in? How many nights are you staying?" He stopped midscan—frozen, eyeing me, with his caterpillar brows quivering like they were trying to sniff out the truth.

I picked at a scab on my elbow. "Oh yeah, I think she told my mom. We're leaving tomorrow anyway."

The caterpillars stopped wiggling and he went back to scanning. "You folks heading over to the Grand Canyon? Are you taking the train over?"

"Uh. Yeah. Isn't that what you do around here?"

"That train ride sure is nice. You can see for miles. Where you from?"

"We're from, um, Wichita." I had always liked how that sounded—Wichita. Who wouldn't want to be from a place called Wichita?

"Is that so? Well, welcome to the Wild West," he said, his caterpillar eyebrows wiggling. "You know, I have a granddaughter about your age. She just loves coming here for a visit. You will certainly love the canyon, except you need to watch out for the diamondback rattlesnakes this season. It's a little cool this year. They're coming out of their hiding places in droves, so watch where you step."

I nodded.

"That will be thirty-six twenty-one. Do you want to charge that to your room?"

My room? Should I charge it to the Lavender Lady's room? I didn't even know how to do that. Didn't she say 202? I couldn't. But . . . No, definitely not.

Instead, I pulled out her money and peeled off two twenty-dollar bills and set them on the counter. The spiders in my stomach quieted. Survival was survival.

He handed me my change. "Do you want a bag for that?"

"Yes." The clock sitting behind the cash register said 10:34. I had to get back to Billie. I grabbed the bag and headed for the front door.

"The rooms are down that way," he said, gesturing toward the hallway. The caterpillars narrowed a titch.

"Oh sorry, I just got turned around," I said.

He relaxed. "I hope your mother feels better."

"She will," I called over my shoulder.

He seemed nice. I bet he was a good grandpa. For a minute, since I was pretending, I imagined he was mine. And Billie and me could live right here at the hotel and go to the Grand Canyon anytime we wanted. For a second, it felt really nice to have a grandpa who was alive instead of dead. But really, I didn't even know if I had one alive grandpa. When I asked Dad about his father, he said he never knew him, so I guess he could still be out there somewhere. He could be anyone, even Caterpillar Eyebrows!

But then my thoughts were interrupted by something amazing. I saw it right out of the corner of my eye. A phone in the hallway! A pay phone sat innocently to my left, like it didn't even know how beautiful it was. Like it didn't even know how it was the answer to all my problems. We could call Julie. I could call her right now and she could come pick us up. No Cowboy. No Dad. No separation. Just me and Billie in our old condo and Julie to take us back to our old life. Except Mom wouldn't be there. But still, it was better than this.

I lifted the black receiver and put it to my ear. Even the dial tone sounded hopeful. Then I remembered Billie, damp, in the shadows, and definitely all alone at the pool. The spiders in my stomach threatened to revolt. I had to get back to her. First, I'd get Billie and then we could call. I ran down the hall, the plastic bag bouncing against my thigh. Nothing mattered, not even rescue, unless I had her.

Survival Strategy #18:
DON'T GET COMFORTABLE

"THESE ARE MY FAVORITE," SAID BILLIE AS she shoved peanut butter crackers into her mouth. Cracker crumbs fell onto her lap. She licked her finger and dabbed them up. If it was possible, the pool felt even quieter than before. We sat on the lounge chair, the one near the broken pool light.

"I-mow," I mumbled, trying not to choke on the three stale-ish mini doughnuts I had shoved into my mouth. I scraped the waxy chocolate off my front teeth with my tongue; probably Caterpillar Eyebrows didn't sell many doughnuts off his shelf. Still, they were good. We hadn't eaten much today. For breakfast, we'd had strawberry Pop-Tarts. But I shoved the memory away.

Only good things now.

Only good things would come to Billie and me. I used my mind powers to make it come true.

Billie held up another package of peanut butter crackers. "Can I have these, too?"

"Of course. Don't I always buy you two when Dad gives me money for food?"

"Yeah."

That was my job. To feed Billie, like my baby bird. Dad didn't want to have to worry about it. He always gave me the money, and I worked it out, usually at a gas station. Sometimes there was a restaurant at a truck stop, but Dad didn't like to go to restaurants. I think too many people.

"You should eat this, too," I said, holding up the turkey jerky. "You need protein."

Billie shook her head.

"You need it, Billie. All animals need it."

"Is it the spicy kind?"

I shook my head.

She grabbed a piece and shoved it in her mouth. "Tell me what else animals need."

I swallowed hard. That was easy. "They need food, shelter, water, most need sun, and . . ." I hesitated and thought about the ants from this morning. All of them with their skinny ant arms dragging that chip across the parking lot, helping one another like a family should. "And they need one another, someone to look after them."

"They do?" asked Billie.

I nodded. Of course they did, didn't they? I guess sea turtles didn't, but I'm sure the mom was sad to leave her eggs.

"How do they look after one another?"

"Like how I watch after you."

She made a face. "I know, but how do animals do it?"

I crumpled my doughnut wrapper into a tiny ball and glanced around the pool. Everything was quiet except for the occasional hum of a machine that sat beside the pool. Tucked behind the hedges, we were safe. And in just a few minutes I was going to call Julie. Now I could almost breathe. I continued, "Well, dolphins talk to other dolphins; like, they tell them where the good fish is or if there is danger."

"How?"

"With clicks and whistles and stuff."

Billie chirped at me through a mouthful of crackers.

"Shh," I said, smiling. She knew dolphins were my favorite. "And killer whales stay together forever—at least the moms and babies do."

"What happens to the dads?"

"They're not allowed."

"Why?"

"I don't know. Maybe they like to be by themselves.

But the moms and babies make a group called a pod and they stay together until they die."

I balled up the peanut butter cracker trash.

She nodded some more, her eyes glistening. "Like us. We're a pod," she whispered. "Except we don't have a mom anymore."

Even if I never talked about Mom, she was always in my brain, floating around, trying to get me to pay attention to her. I wondered if Billie was thinking about that awful day like I was.

Survival Strategy #19:
NEVER ANSWER THE DOOR

ON THAT DAY THE KNOCKING ON THE DOOR was really loud. And our babysitter, Mrs. Mason, didn't hear it because she had fallen asleep watching the cooking channel again.

It was Saturday morning, and Mom was supposed to be home any minute from her night shift at the hospital, and she said she would take Billie and me to the beach that day. So I didn't care that Mrs. Mason was starting to drool onto her sweatshirt. Or that the baked crème brûlée French toast on TV looked so good that I might drool, too.

The knocking wouldn't stop, so I answered the door.

And if I was smart—and usually I am pretty smart—I would have left that door closed. And I would've let those policemen sit on the porch forever. Because then I'd never have to hear what they were going to say. And Billie wouldn't have to know, either. She was eating breakfast—Cocoa Puffs and Lucky Charms mixed together.

We didn't know what would happen when that door opened.

When it did, Mrs. Mason woke up. And a shortish policeman with sunglasses told her first. Because she's an adult. And the big one with a mustache wouldn't even look at Billie or me, but after they talked to Mrs. Mason, they said that Mom had been in a serious accident and that we needed to go to the hospital at once.

And Mrs. Mason cried, which made me mad. Because it wasn't her mom. It wasn't someone she loved. It wasn't her world being sucked down into a tornado.

Mrs. Mason cried and said, "Oh my."

I didn't. Not then. Not yet.

And Billie said, "I can't leave," because she didn't understand. She whined when we got into Mrs. Mason's old Cadillac to drive to the hospital. She had said, "My cereal's getting soggy."

Now, thinking about it didn't change anything; it just made my chest hurt.

I went over a list of rattlesnake facts in my head.

1. Live in deserts and mountains.
2. Hibernate in winter.
3. Give birth to eight to ten snakes at once.
4. Baby rattlesnakes' rattles don't work.
5. Baby rattlesnakes are more aggressive than adults and more deadly.

When Mom died, it was fast. Almost like stepping on a rattlesnake. Except it wasn't a snake that got her; it was an Explorer. She was hit crossing the road by a car called a Ford Explorer. Then she was gone forever.

She was already gone when we got to the hospital. At first the doctor wouldn't let me see her. But Mrs. Mason insisted. So they let me, even though it was not a very pretty thing to see. But I had to do it. Mrs. Mason said closure. But after I said good-bye, I wouldn't let Billie see her face, only her feet. I didn't want Mom's bruised and bloodied face to be the last thing Billie remembered about her. She didn't even look like herself. I wished it wasn't the last thing I remembered.

Dead. Deadly. Deadliest.

Now the machine by the hotel pool made a whirring noise again.

"Come on, Billie. We've got to go," I said as I gathered

our trash and stuffed it into the concrete trash can near the pool.

Billie wiped her eyes and yawned. She tucked her knees up to her chin, stretching the towel over her legs. "She's here, Liberty. Even though you can't see her, I know she's watching us."

I looked up at the sky. A few small stars began to appear, probably planets, across the bluish dark. And the full moon blinked at me. Was Mom really there? It didn't matter, because I was the one who had to save us.

I grabbed Billie's clothes off the cement and shook them hard. They were still damp and smelled like chlorine, but they would have to do.

"Put these on," I said, trying to shove her head through the bottom of the sweatshirt.

"They're wet," she whined.

"Just a little," I whispered. "And be quiet. Our voices echo out here." I pushed her feet into her shorts and pulled them up over her.

"I don't want to wear these," Billie said, getting that stubborn look.

"Billie, it's all we have."

Just then, I heard footsteps.

I pulled Billie toward the hedges where we had our little picnic camp and covered her mouth.

We inched toward the empty space between the hedge

and the fence as the footsteps got closer. Then they stopped.

I held my breath. An orca can hold its breath for five minutes; if you think about it, five minutes is a real long time. Soon the footsteps began again—*click-click-click*, moving farther away from where Billie and me huddled into each other. Sometimes I needed a reminder of how important our little pod was and that I couldn't let it break up over anything.

"Come on. I saw a phone," I whispered. "We're going to call Julie."

Survival Strategy #20:
PANIC IS NOT YOUR FRIEND

THE PAY PHONE HALLWAY WAS COOL AND silent. My notebook had gotten wet at the pool. The corners were fat and bloated. Some of the ink was smudged like a bruise, and the pages stuck together. But I found the page I was looking for.

"Here, you hold it and tell me the number when I ask," I said to Billie, pointing to the numbers on the page.

She nodded solemnly.

Then I fumbled around in the plastic shopping bag for the change Caterpillar Eyebrows had given me. The coins were slippery and warm, and I had no idea how much money I really needed. Each quarter made a loud plunk as I dropped it in the narrow slot. The nest of spiders in my stomach churned.

What if she didn't answer? What if she said no? What if—

"Tell me the number," I hissed as I scanned the hallway for movement. No one was at the front desk when we had walked in.

I punched in the numbers. A voice said, "Please deposit twenty-five cents."

I couldn't reach the bag at my feet. "Billie, dump the bag out. Look for some more quarters."

Billie turned it upside down.

"Please deposit twenty-five cents," repeated the nasal recording.

"Billie!"

"Here." She slapped some coins in my hand.

I deposited the money and waited. Was it calling Julie? The crease between Billie's eyes deepened. Then the phone began to ring.

Billie pulled on my T-shirt. "Let me talk to her. I want to tell her something."

I couldn't concentrate. "Stop it," I said. "Quit pulling on me."

Suddenly, it was Julie's voice.

"Julie. It's-me-Liberty-and-Billie-and-we're-here-in-Arizona-I-think-and-Dad-left-us-and-we-need-you-to-come-and-get-us-because-we-don't-know-where-he-is—"

". . . leave a message after the beep," and she was gone. I hadn't expected not to talk to her.

I speed-talked a message into her cell phone. "Julie, it's me, Liberty. We're at a hotel. And Dad's gone. We can't find him. You need to come and—" The voice mail cut me off. The disappointment was so thick, like a mist. I could barely breathe.

"I wanted to talk to her," said Billie, her eyes desperate and tired. It was past eleven. "You said I could talk to her!"

"No, I didn't." I knelt down and picked up my note-book and our money that had been dumped at my feet. I shoved it all back into the bag.

Tears rolled down Billie's face. "You said," she whis-pered, pointing a skinny finger at me. "You said we were going home. You said I could talk to her." Her warm breath mixed in with the disappointment floating in the air like skunk spray.

From around the corner, there was a loud bang. Some-one must be back manning the desk.

"Come on," I said, pulling Billie's arm, dragging her to the end of the hall and the exit, back to the swimming pool.

Billie lay down right on the dirty carpet. I pulled on her arm, but she was like a fat seal at SeaWorld, deter-mined not to move an inch. "You said," she said, crying even harder.

This was what I was supposed to avoid. Mom always said a Billie meltdown should be registered on the Richter scale. But I could never predict when they would come.

A man opened his room door, his eyes red and blurry, like we had interrupted his nice sleep.

"Sorry," I said, my face hot. "My sister forgot her teddy bear in the car. She's just upset."

I pulled her arms and dragged her down the hall.

"You promised!" Billie yelled, her face as red as the ants I saw this morning.

The man scowled.

With my hip, I pushed the door open and tried to get her outside, but Billie hung on to the door frame and screamed, "You said we were going home! You said we were leaving *right now*!"

A line of sweat rolled down my neck.

The man folded his arms, his scowl mixed with a glare. "Some people are trying to sleep."

"I'm sorry. We're leaving," I said, because now he was standing outside his room in the hallway. "She's fine. Go back to bed." I lugged Billie up into my arms like she was a huge baby and stepped outside, the door still propped against my hip. The man's eyes turned into narrow slits as he slammed his door.

Then Billie slipped onto the concrete and lay there in

a heap. Her voice was quieter, but raw. "I want to go home. Where's Daddy?"

I pulled her back up into a cradle like I had super strength and headed toward the pool. "I've got you, Billie. Don't you worry about anything."

Survival Strategy #21:

BE PATIENT, LIKE A SNAPPING TURTLE

"ARE YOU OKAY NOW?" I ASKED, PULLING the towel even tighter around Billie's shoulders. I stroked her arm, pretending that of course she was okay. She had to be.

Finally, she nodded.

"Do you want to hear some animal facts?" I asked.

She nodded again, eyes closed, her breathing slow. Only then could I let go of the worry pinched between my shoulder blades. Billie had to listen to me. She had to do what I said and she couldn't act crazy like that or we would get in so much trouble.

Billie's eyes opened just a crack.

"All right," I whispered, flipping the pages in my notebook.

I found what I was looking for: the North American snapping turtle. I stopped patting Billie's arm and took a deep breath. "The snapping turtle is one of the cleverest turtles on the planet," I said, trying to make the facts sound like a bedtime story. "It uses camouflage to catch prey. It sits in a pond, just like an ordinary rock, and waits for dinner to come."

Billie's eyes closed again.

"Frogs and fish are the snapping turtle's favorite meals. Snapping turtles are patient, because they have to be. Otherwise they would go hungry. The turtle sits with its little face poking out from under the water until a frog hops by, and then *bam!*"

Billie flinched.

So I spoke even more quietly. "He grabs the frog and slurps it into a juicy meal."

Billie rolled onto her side, her shoulders moving up and down with each breath, asleep.

I stood and scooted the other lounge chair closer to Billie's and lay down so near I could smell the chlorine in her hair. I shut my eyes, willing myself to sleep, but now, even though I was so tired, I couldn't. What-ifs kept charging across my brain. What if someone came while we were sleeping? What if that man in the hallway complained? What if Julie never answered her phone? What if something bad had happened to her like it happened to Mom?

Billie turned over in her sleep and said, "Daddy." Almost every night she talked in her sleep.

If only Dad knew how much we wanted to love him.

I swung my legs off the lounge chair and placed my feet quietly on the scratchy concrete. I grabbed my notebook and pulled the pen out of the spine. It fell open to a page I hadn't looked at in a while. *Dad* was written across the top. Underneath was a place I reserved for everything I knew about my dad. I started it maybe a year ago. Still, it wasn't a very long list, but it had a photo I liked.

I smoothed the picture of the gentoo penguin taken by Dad in Antarctica. The penguin stared back at me. I hadn't really noticed it before, but the penguin looked pretty sad.

I had found the penguin picture hidden in a box under Mom's bed when I was eight. I wasn't trying to be nosy; I was only looking for a shoe-box home for a monarch caterpillar I had caught. The babysitter was watching TV. Mom was at work, like always. And usually she didn't care if Billie and me were in her bedroom. I opened the box, and at first it didn't seem interesting, but then I saw an old picture of Dad and me. I was probably four. And there were a few others of Dad with Billie as a baby, and Mom before she had us.

Also, there were pictures of animals clipped from magazines. As I looked closer, I realized they were Dad's pictures! Every single one taken by Sam Marshall. He was in India, Australia, the Amazon, Costa Rica, and Antarctica. Now I knew where Dad was! It was the best prize ever, like I had found him at the end of a rainbow.

I set the box on the kitchen table and waited for Mom to get home.

When she walked in the door, I said, "I thought you didn't know where Dad was."

"I don't know where he is," she snapped. She looked real tired, and her scrubs had maybe dried blood on the corner.

"But it says on this picture that he was in Antarctica," I said, showing her the gentoo penguin picture.

She plucked it out of my hand. "This was from a year ago. And before that, it probably took six months to print."

I grabbed it back. "I want to write him a letter. Or I could probably try to e-mail him at this magazine."

She flung open the refrigerator door. "I already tried that, Liberty. Don't waste your time."

"But . . ." I pushed the tears out of my eyes.

Mom closed the door and put her arm around me. "I'm

just trying to help you so you don't get your hopes up, Liberty. That's my job. I'm your mom."

"I know," I said. "But I just . . ." I folded the picture in half. How could I say what I really wanted without making Mom feel bad? I just wanted Dad.

"Go write your letter," she said. "I'll send it for you."

I wrote ten letters and sent three e-mails, but I never heard from him.

I didn't like to think about that.

Now the stars were coming out, and Billie mumbled again in her sleep. I went over and sat down next to her on her chair and patted her back. Just thinking about Dad and Billie and about what happened this morning made my chest feel tight. I rubbed the sore space between my heart and my rib cage, but the aching only got worse. I looked up at the sky again.

Breathe, Liberty.

Billie sighed.

Was Mom really there like Billie thought? It didn't matter—but it made me feel better to think her soul cells were still floating around in the atmosphere. Right now, the bigger questions were about people who had real heartbeats and living cells. Where was Dad? Happy to be alone in his camper so he could take pictures of things that didn't talk or eat or cry? Would Julie get my message?

I turned to a fresh piece of paper in my notebook.

I angled the page under a stream of light coming from the hotel and wrote across the top *MY PLAN*. Then I scratched it out and wrote *OUR PLAN*. I wrote out my list and hoped this would keep the panic away, because fear slowly stalked around in my chest, ready to split me in two, just like a Bengal tiger. All I needed was to stay calm and keep Billie calm, too; otherwise we were nothing but prey.

Survival Strategy #22:

IF YOU LOOK HARD ENOUGH, YOU CAN FIND ALMOST NORMAL

WHEN DAD, BILLIE, AND ME WERE IN THE desert, it was hot, like sweat-in-your-eyes-and-in-between-your-toes hot. And I couldn't help but wonder about Antonio and how he was probably, at that very moment, playing at the beach with his brother, Salvy. Antonio had said Dad would bring us back after a few days because living in a camper with two loco girls all summer would get old. And anyway, we'd get bored. But those weeks had turned into a month. Dad still hadn't brought us back, but Antonio was right about one thing.

We were bored.

And I wasn't so sure that Dad wasn't all those things Antonio's mom had said. Because he did like it quiet. And he did like to be alone.

Would I ever play king of the island on top of mountains of sand again? Would I ever get to make s'mores over gigantic bonfires? Mom loved to make them with a peanut butter cup slid in between the graham crackers.

Sometimes Dad made a fire, but we hadn't had s'mores yet. I wanted bonfires. And Mom. And so did Billie. At night when we were supposed to be asleep, we whispered about stuff. Stuff like Mom and the ocean and home. And how maybe we should call Julie. She said we could. But somehow that felt like giving in. We *had* to make it work with Dad, because what would happen if we didn't? Would Julie keep us?

Then Dad would say, "Go to sleep."

And I guess he wanted someone to sleep, because after the first few weeks he hardly ever did. He was always driving, reading, or working. But hardly ever sleeping. All animals needed to sleep, even the nocturnal ones. But not Dad.

Our camper had pulled into a camping spot early one morning in Arizona, a month after he picked us up. Dad had been driving all night, but now he was finally asleep in his bed. So Billie and me ate Pop-Tarts and played Go

Fish. And I made her brush her teeth. And I brushed, too, spitting into a paper cup sitting on the counter.

"What did the ocean say to the sand?" I asked Billie.

She shrugged, wiping the spit from her mouth.

"I mist you."

She stared.

"Get it? Mist, like mist from the ocean?"

"Yeah, I get it."

She arranged Koala nicely on my pillow. "I miss the ocean."

At this campsite, it was magma-hot already and only nine o'clock in the morning. I opened the window to let in some air and the screen fell out, landing in the dirt. I went to get it, and when I opened the door, I heard something. A twittering and chirping, but like a million times louder than it should be.

Billie poked her head out of the window. "What is that?"

"I don't know. It sounds like . . . birds."

Billie climbed out of the camper and we followed the noise toward the red cliffs ahead. And as we got closer, we could see nests, thousands of round, muddy nests, almost smashed on top of one another, hanging on to the side of the cliff like barnacles on a ship. Birds flitted and squawked and fought, darting in and out of nests, not even noticing us as we crept closer and closer.

"Wow," said Billie, all shiny and breathless. "A bird city."

"I know," I said, even though I hadn't seen anything like that, not even on Animal Planet. And I held my breath, because what if they all disappeared right before my eyes like a dream?

"What are you two doing out here?" asked Dad, coming up behind us quiet as a cheetah. But he had his camera around his neck and he didn't look mad. He was staring at the birds with the same look of wonder Billie had.

"We heard them," said Billie.

"I've never seen so many cliff swallows all at once." Dad stared at the mountain. "There must be thousands."

He brought the camera up to his eye, and soon I heard the familiar click as he tried to capture the magic of Bird City.

"Billie," he said. "Run back and get my tripod. I left it on my bed."

Billie looked at me and then back at Dad. Usually, he didn't like us to touch his stuff.

Dad pulled the camera away from his face. "Quickly. I don't want to miss the best shots."

I nodded at her and started to follow, because that tripod was pretty heavy. I carried it up the trail the last time Dad took us with him, and it was seriously heavy.

But Dad said, "Take a look, Liberty." He held out his camera to me.

Dad had never offered to let me look through his camera before. And I was kind of afraid to touch it, because what if I touched the wrong thing or smudged it or broke it or—

"Here," he said, still holding it out to me. "You've got to see these eggs." His left eye squinted so I could barely see his eyelashes poking out.

I inched my face toward the viewfinder as Dad held it so I could see. And then I saw them, like I was standing only inches away. Little white eggs with black speckles, just like the chocolate eggs Mom used to put in my Easter basket . . . except these were definitely not chocolate.

They were beautiful.

And real.

And loved.

I could see that right away, because of all the mom and dad birds circling-spinning-darting-protecting each and every egg.

"Can you see them?" asked Dad. He was closer than I'd ever been to him before. He smelled like dirty hair. "Everything looks better through a camera," he said. I knew what he meant. The eggs were so sharp. So clear. Like I could reach out and touch them if I wanted.

"Here," said Billie, thunking the tripod down at Dad's feet. She was breathing hard. She must have run the whole way just to make him happy. But it worked, because he smiled and pointed the camera at her.

"Picture perfect," he said.

Billie smiled as Dad took her picture.

"Do you know how much I paid for this camera? Thousands of dollars. It makes everything look amazing. And this lens—see how it makes the depth of field go on forever?" he asked.

I looked through the viewfinder again.

There was Billie. Beautiful. Golden. Strawberry Pop-Tart smudged on her top lip. The sunlight bright behind her.

"The trick is in the camera," said Dad, pulling his worth-all-the-money camera away and aiming it back at the swallows, which didn't seem so interesting now. "The camera and the photographer make a perfect marriage," he said.

And I wanted to say, *No. It's not a photography trick. It's just Billie. Perfect Billie.*

Mom could always see it. Why couldn't he?

Survival Strategy #23:
BLEND IN

THE SMELL OF FOOD—REAL, DELICIOUS, cooked food—woke me from where I lay in an awkward heap, deposited at the foot of Billie's lounge chair. For a moment my heart bumped. But there she was, still curled into a ball under the towel. I stood, stretched, and picked a piece of grass off my cheek. The sky seemed to brighten even in the minute I stood there, but there was no actual sun out yet.

I moved to where I could see Billie's face. Her worry crease looked deeper. I reached to trace it with my finger, but hesitated. Maybe she was happy somewhere inside a dream where Mom was alive and being left at the gas station was nothing but a make-believe story.

Finally, I shook her arm gently. "Billie, it's time to get up."

She groaned. "Not yet."

It was still early, six thirty. But I felt naked with the rows of blank windows facing the pool where we sat so exposed. In the daylight this would not be considered a proper hideaway for any self-respecting animal.

"Billie, come on. Let's get breakfast."

She popped up, a tangled mass of white hair. It swayed with each turn of her head. I couldn't help but smile. "Come here," I said. "Let me fix your hair."

Billie stood and staggered toward me, her face still mashed with lines from the towel. I knew food would inspire her.

I pulled the plastic bag with our money, leftover food, and my notebook closer to me. Just knowing I had a plan already made me feel better. More like a predator than prey.

I combed her hair with my fingers, doused with some pool water. Like magic, I turned her bed head into a messy bun with the elastic from around my wrist. "There," I said, trying to test her mood. "You are ready for the royal feast."

Please, Billie, no meltdowns today, please.

She stuck her tongue out, but the corners of her mouth turned up into a small smile.

I turned my attention to how I looked, trying to erase

any sign that I had taken a bath in an over-chlorinated pool and slept in my clothes all night. I slicked my hair into a tight ponytail and asked Billie, "How old do you think I am?"

Billie, still grumpy, but not yet at meltdown level, looked at me like I was crazy. "You're twelve," she said.

"I know." But I was tall for my age, which was one of the top three things people said when they met me. The other two were that I looked like my mom and that I acted mature for my age. Of course I did. Mom worked almost all the time. How else was I supposed to act? I hoped I could pass for fourteen, maybe. "But how old do I *look*?"

Billie shrugged. "Old."

"Okay, come on," I said after I counted our money. I guess if I couldn't get ahold of Julie, maybe we could take a bus back to San Diego, if buses stopped here. Didn't everyone want to see the Grand Canyon, especially bus people?

Billie stuck the army man she'd found by the pool in her pocket and followed me as we slipped silently through the wide space in the fence. I didn't want to draw attention to the fact that she was being so well behaved, so I left it alone. She was like the skittish sagebrush lizard we saw at Zion and I didn't want to spook her.

The slap of my shoes, plus Billie's bare foot, echoed in the empty morning air, reminding me how important it was for us to blend in. We were guests at the hotel, like every other person here. I took a deep breath. I could pretend. Faking it had become my specialty.

I gave my notebook list from last night a mental check.

1. Free continental breakfast—like Caterpillar Eyebrows said.
2. Call Julie again.
3.

Three was to be determined. Number three depended on how number two went. And of course, I couldn't accomplish number two if Billie threw a fit again. And she was most likely not to throw a fit if she was nice and full. But first, we had to find a bathroom.

After a stop in the bathroom, we were ready to eat. The smell of cinnamon and coffee filled the air, making the breakfast easy to find. It was set up in a large room near the front desk. In the center of the room sat a long table full of doughnuts, bagels, pastries, yogurt, cold cereal, fruit, juice, and pots of steaming something. My stomach gurgled. I planted Billie at a table where I could keep an eye on her, but also where I could hide her a little so people couldn't see her feet. Surprisingly, there were a few families already there, dressed in shorts and T-shirts and hiking sandals, I guessed ready to get a jump on exploring the Grand Canyon.

Billie's eyes wandered hungrily toward the food.

"Stay put," I said. "I'll get your food."

Billie shook her head.

"Stay," I said. "You don't have a shoe."

"Okay," she mumbled.

I filled one plate with doughnuts and pastries and another with fruit and yogurt and set them both down in front of Billie. Next, I filled two bowls with steaming cinnamon oatmeal, chock-full of raisins and apples. It smelled so good. It took almost all of my self-control not to set the bowl down right there and lap it up like a dog. The bowls teetered a bit as I tried to balance one on top of the other. A largish lady in an apron pushed past me.

"Hungry?" she asked, eyeing my heaping bowls.

I nodded.

She added more blueberry muffins to the muffin tray and then wiped her hands on her apron. "Here, let me help you with that," she said, reaching for a bowl.

"I'm all right," I said, pulling them toward me.

"Don't be silly. That's my job." She plucked the oatmeal from my hands and gave me a cheery smile. "Now, where are you seated?"

I pointed to Billie. "Right there, with my little sister."

Obediently, I followed Apron Lady.

She set our bowls on the table. "Why, hello there," she said to Billie. "Are you enjoying your breakfast this morning?"

Billie nodded, her mouth overflowing with pastry.

"That's nice. We aim to please." She smiled again, looking around the room for our parents, I imagined.

I smiled and waved at an older man who balanced three muffins on a plate, hoping she would think he was our dad. "Thanks so much," I said to the lady.

Apron Lady glanced at the man and then at us; I could almost see her computing everything in her brain. Then, as if everything checked out okay, she smiled at me. "Well, let me know if I can get you anything else."

"Okay," I said, my eyes following her back to the buffet table as she arranged more muffins. Just being here around all these people made me nervous.

"So good," said Billie between mouthfuls.

I pushed a bowl of oatmeal toward her. "Here, eat this, too. It's good for you."

Billie stuffed another piece of banana into her mouth, so blissful in the land of Endless Breakfast that she barely noticed me. She was actually humming.

I reached down into our plastic bag, grabbed the coins floating around the bottom, and stuck them in my pocket.

"Billie," I said. I shoved another spoonful of oatmeal into my mouth and swallowed. "Billie."

"What?"

"I've got to go to the bathroom. I'll be right back."

She nodded, not even questioning that we had just been in the bathroom. This was the perfect time for me to call Julie without Billie getting hyperdramatic. I grabbed my notebook from under the table. After last night's meltdown I had tried to memorize Julie's phone number, but I still needed it, just in case my brain wouldn't cooperate.

The phone was just around the corner, so while dialing I kept my ears pricked up for anything unusual going on in the breakfast room. Billie would surely make noise if anyone bothered her. I dialed Julie's cell phone number again and my stomach began to churn—the oatmeal I had just put inside threatened to come out.

Please be there.

It rang and then picked up, but the same thing happened as the night before. Julie's cheerful voice on the voice mail telling me to leave her a message and she'd call me back. For a second I wanted to cry, just like Billie, but then the phone beeped and I knew I had to do a better job of leaving her information than I had last night. I opened my notebook to where I had stuck a free map

I picked up near the front desk. Sometimes the best strategy is to be prepared, so I told her exactly where we were, even the telephone number of the hotel, before the voice mail cut off.

Then I called her home phone and left another message. I had covered everything. There was no way she could miss my messages.

I hung the phone in the cradle. It was fine. Everything was fine. Julie always had her cell phone except when she was at work; she was probably working a night shift or something. I should feel satisfied now that someone knew we were here. Someone who would come and find us. I should feel so much better—so why didn't I? After two months in the desert with my dad, I was beginning to recognize that feeling of uneasiness, like someone had drawn a crooked line along my spine with a stretched, cold finger. Instinct was trying to tell me something.

I stared at the breakfast room door, worried that something had happened to Billie. I spun around and bumped straight into someone sitting behind me in a wheelchair. Someone I couldn't possibly forget. It was Orson, like a huge roasted marshmallow, wrinkled and brown; he sat just staring at me.

And right behind him was the Lavender Lady.

"Excuse me," I stuttered, trying to get out of their way.

The Lavender Lady didn't even glance in my direction;

she was too busy marching toward the front desk. But Orson's cloudy eyes locked onto mine, like an owl with night vision capability, but instead of seeing in the dark, he could see right into me. Like he knew everything—the hijacked car ride, the pee, the stolen money. Somehow he knew it all.

I took a step back, trying to camouflage myself with a potted plant.

The Lavender Lady pushed his wheelchair past me and parked it near the front desk, but Orson's head wrenched back, staring, not letting me free. Slowly, I inched toward the door.

The Lavender Lady slammed her hand on the front desk. "I demand to see the manager," she declared to the teenager reading a book behind the counter.

The girl jumped. "My manager's not in right now." She closed the book, but held her place with her finger. "Is there anything I can help you with?"

"There most certainly is! I've been robbed. I'm certain it was one of your employees."

The potted plant behind me tipped over. The Lavender Lady barely noticed. But Orson still stared.

The girl behind the counter dropped her book and glanced around in a panic. "Hold on a sec," she said, before she disappeared behind the counter where the little door was. I set the pot upright, scooped up the dirt, and dumped it back in. All the while, my cheeks and face burned. How could I sit here and let her accuse someone else of stealing when I knew that most of her money, the part I hadn't spent yet, sat in a plastic bag underneath Billie's dirty feet?

"They're getting the manager," the Lavender Lady said to Orson.

Orson turned to her and mumbled something.

"Manager," she said again.

Orson looked agitated. He stared at me, and his mouth formed words only he could understand.

The Lavender Lady's lips set into a grim line as she tucked her purse tightly beneath her arm. I felt sorry for the girl behind the counter, but there was no way I wanted the Lavender Lady's anger beam pointed at me.

Orson raised his arm in my direction, mumbling louder.

The Lavender Lady patted his shoulder. "I know this is upsetting, but we're just going to wait and get this whole thing sorted out. *Orson. Just wait."*

Survival Strategy #24:
RUN

I RAN INTO THE BREAKFAST ROOM, ALMOST knocking into two kids at the juice machine, and slid into my seat next to Billie. My heart thumped so violently that it felt like it might jump right out onto her almost empty plate. Billie glanced at me and then at her plate, disgusted, like its near emptiness was my fault.

"What took you so long?" she asked.

"Nothing."

"Get me another blueberry muffin," she said, like she was the queen of everything.

I stared at the door, waiting for the Lavender Lady to come charging through to shake me until I had returned every cent of her money.

"Another muffin," demanded Billie.

I glanced at her. "You've had enough. No more muffins. Come on," I said, pulling on her arm. "We've got to go."

"What? Why? I'm not finished."

"Yes you are. That's, like, your third plate. Hurry," I hissed as I pulled her out of her seat.

"No!" said Billie. "I'm not ready yet. Who made you the boss?"

People were beginning to stare.

I sat back down. "Billie, stop it. You know why I'm in charge. I'm older."

Billie played with a kiwi on her plate, her eyebrows pushed down low over her eyes. "It's not fair," she said. "You're so bossy."

I should have sat and listened. I should have been patient. I should have just let her have her way. But then a man walked up to our table. At first I didn't recognize him, but when I imagined him in a bathrobe with messed-up hair, then I knew exactly who he was: the guy we woke up last night in the hallway when Billie screamed like a howler monkey.

"Aren't you the girls I saw last night in the hallway?" he asked, squinting to get a better look at us.

I pretended he wasn't there.

Billie looked pale.

"Yes," he said, as if he had made a decision. "It was you."

He looked around the breakfast room, his eyes narrowing. "I'd like to speak to your parents."

I stared at the white carnation on the table, tucked between the salt and pepper, and willed him to disappear.

"Which ones are they?" he asked, scanning the room.

I jumped up. "You can't."

"Oh, really?" His face twisted into an awkward smile, like his lips weren't used to being happy. "And why not?"

"Because they went to the bathroom," I said, hoping I sounded believable.

He folded his arms across his chest. "Then I'll just wait." He smirked and stood right in front of our table, so close I could smell the coffee and cigarettes on his breath.

Suddenly, Apron Lady was there, standing right next to the man with her arms folded over her large, aproned chest. "Can I help you?" she asked. She was as wide as he was tall, so she felt more intimidating.

"I don't think so," he said, still trying to look friendly, but the way he grasped the spoon in his right hand wouldn't let me believe it.

"I'll be the judge of that. What are you doing with these girls?"

He ran his hands through his hair, his smile now gone, replaced by a sneer. "I'm waiting to speak to these girls' parents. Last night they woke me up in the middle of the night screaming and carrying on in the hallway. I want to have a few words with the people who let their children run around like wild animals. In. The. Middle. Of. The. Night!" He jabbed the air with his spoon just for emphasis.

Apron Lady turned and bent low to face Billie and me. "Is this true?" she asked, like he had just accused us of landing a spaceship in the parking lot.

I shook my head.

Billie nodded.

I stood now, my legs jelly, and pointed at Billie. "We were . . ." My arm shook as I stretched it toward the man. "He was . . ."

Billie now stood right behind me, her face buried in my T-shirt.

Apron Lady looked at me with worry in her eyes, laced with a smidgen of curiosity. I should tell her what happened to Billie and me. About being left by Dad. About being all alone. Maybe I could.

"I . . ." I hesitated, my body vibrating with adrenaline.

"If you don't do something about this reckless behavior in your hotel, then I certainly will," interrupted the man, grabbing hold of my arm. "I'm not leaving until I've talked to this girl's parents."

And just in that moment, I made a choice, like many hunted animals do, acting out of pure instinct. First, I kicked the man in the knee as hard as I could. Second, I grabbed Billie by the hand.

"Oh, oh, oh!" he yelled as his knees buckled and he fell to the floor. And just for a split second, out of the corner of my eye, I saw pure shock on Apron Lady's face as we bolted out of the breakfast room and into the lobby where the Lavender Lady still sat complaining to a brand-new person holding an official-looking clipboard. Everyone turned and stared.

"Run!" I yelled to Billie over my shoulder.

She stumbled and tripped as I pulled her behind me, my grip like a boa constrictor's. We tumbled through the front door and ran for the road that welcomed us back with a sun-scorched hello. Our reply was the sound of Billie's one bare foot as it slapped the pavement.

Survival Strategy #25:
HIDE

"STOP," SAID BILLIE AFTER ABOUT FIVE minutes of sprinting. She was panting so hard, I could barely understand her. *"Pleeease,"* she said, falling onto her knees, sucking in huge gulps of air.

I slowed down. There was no noise of anyone chasing after us—no yelling, or running, or pounding feet. So I stopped, too, throwing myself down next to her on the little patch of grass in front of a Texaco gas station.

Billie lay facedown in the grass, mumbling something.

"What?" I asked, crawling closer. Still worried there were people after us, I looked down the sidewalk in the direction of the hotel, but a large group of hedges made it impossible to see. But I couldn't hear anyone. And I couldn't get that man's creepy smile out of my mind. Why was he so determined to get us in trouble? The press of his fingers still haunted my arm.

Billie mumbled again.

"What?" I asked, pulling her over so I could hear.

She was as red as a Starburst. She pulled some grass out of her mouth. "When's Julie coming?"

She looked so pathetic, I couldn't possibly tell her I didn't know. "Soon."

"When?" she asked.

"Pretty soon."

Then I heard the clack of footsteps coming down the sidewalk from where we had been. "Come on," I said, pulling Billie up.

"What?"

"Someone's coming."

Now I could see legs and shoes. Tan pants and black shiny shoes. Was it that guy from the hotel? I couldn't remember what he was wearing—only the spoon he had held in his hand.

"Come on," I whispered. Billie and I jogged toward the side of the gas station building and hid behind a parked car.

Billie's face was pinched, just like when the doctor had told us about Mom. I was so tired of that look on her face, I could hardly stand it.

"I'm sure it's just a random person," I said, forcing a

smile and trying to make my voice sound happy. "I'm just being safe, okay?"

Billie nodded, peering at the sidewalk from behind me.

Then he appeared. His hands were on his hips as he glared down the road, then at the sidewalk, and finally he scowled at the gas station. His eyes zeroed in on the car we hid behind. It was him. The crazy Spoon Guy from the hotel.

I pulled Billie back against the wall. "I can't believe it," I said.

"Believe what?" asked Billie.

I guided her toward the back of the gas station. "It's that guy from the hotel."

"It is?" Now her face was even more petrified. What was I thinking, telling her that?

We turned and slunk down along the wall until we were directly behind the gas station, hopefully camou-flaged by the shade.

"Watch out," I said, pointing to a pool of black stuff right beside our feet.

Billie nodded.

Once we were out of the Spoon Guy's line of sight, my heart began to return to normal. He wouldn't come all the way back here just to look for us. Would he?

Animals on the run need to use everything in their en-vironment to help themselves. The gas station parking lot was next to some apartment buildings. My fingers itched for my notebook, tucked in my back pocket, so I could plan our next move, but we had no time. There was:

1. A guy fiddling with his tires near a machine that said AIR.
2. Some kid about my age riding his bike around in circles.
3. A black semitruck with its hood open, pulled over to the side.

Painted on the door of the semitruck was FIRE BROTHERS TRUCKING—BARSTOW, CA, with bright, beautiful flames circling around the words, like the whole thing just might catch on fire. The door to the cab sat open, and I couldn't see anyone inside.

Billie waved at the kid on the bike.

"Stop that," I said, pulling her arm down.

She stared at her feet and whispered, "He waved at me first."

The kid smiled at us, his legs pumping harder as he cruised around the guy putting air in his tires.

"We don't wave at strangers."

"You did at breakfast."

"No, I didn't." Then I remembered waving at the man with the muffins. "Well, that was different; that guy didn't even see me, and I had to wave to pretend he was our . . ." I stopped.

Billie sometimes seemed so much younger than she actually was.

"You're right," I said. "I did wave. But I shouldn't have. So let's just say that we're not going to wave at or talk to strangers, okay?" That seemed to satisfy her.

The kid now rode his bike closer to where we sat. The rusty chain let out a huge squeal.

"Hey," he said, stopping the bike two feet from us. A smear of dirt sat above his right eyebrow.

I stared straight ahead and pretended he wasn't there.

"Hi," said Billie.

"Billie," I hissed. "What did I just say?"

She shrugged, her face turning red.

"What's up?" the boy asked. He had a thicket of red hair that grew in all different directions. His face was sprinkled with freckles. He jiggled his knee like he needed to use the bathroom. And it was getting harder to pretend he wasn't there.

"Don't you talk?" he asked me, rubbing sweat out of his eyes, right into the smear of dirt. "Well, I know you do, 'cause I heard you talking to her." He pointed a meaty finger wrapped in a Band-Aid at Billie.

"Don't you know it's rude to point?" I asked.

His arm came down to his side. He wiped his hand

on his Star Wars T-shirt and shrugged his shoulders in a way that reminded me of a five-year-old, even though he looked about my age.

Go away.

But still he wouldn't leave. He glanced at the guy working on the semi, trying to look bored.

The semi guy had the most tattoos I had ever seen. On his arm was a picture of a tongue with a ring pierced through the center. It made me shudder just to look at it. He walked around to the front of his truck, and then half of him disappeared under the hood.

"What are you doing?" the boy asked, turning back toward us. The freckles on his face turned a deep shade of red.

Billie just smiled.

"Nothing," I said.

He shrugged in his annoying way and stared back at us, chewing a huge wad of gum.

"And anyway, it's none of your business what we're doing," I said.

"Okay. What happened to her shoe?" he asked, his foot fiddling with the bike pedal.

"It broke," said Billie.

"You should get another one."

"Yeah, we know. Thanks a lot," I said, turning my back away from him, hoping he would take the hint.

Still he stayed.

I pulled Billie closer to me.

Then he said, "So, do you guys want to do something?"

"Yeah," said Billie.

I pushed up off the ground, completely exasperated, wishing I did have bearded dragon spikes to wave around and tell him to leave. "Of course not," I said. "Go away."

He shrugged, completely unfazed. He looked in the direction of the apartment buildings, then he blew a big bubble. When it popped he said, "Well, why are you just sitting here? What *are* you doing?"

Slowly, an idea formed.

"We're hiding," I said. Sometimes even animals help one another. Like the dolphin that led a whale and its baby out of too shallow water. Sometimes they help.

"From who?" he asked, leaning in closer, super happy to be let in on the secret.

"Some weird guy," I said. "He's at the gas station and he's totally creeping us out."

The boy nodded, like creepy gas station guys were a normal thing. He pulled out a pack of gum from his pocket. "Do you want a piece?"

"No," I said.

Billie nodded. She shoved the square of purple gum into her mouth, her jaws struggling to chomp down on it. Finally, she got it going and blew a huge bubble.

"You sure?" he asked, holding out a cube to me.

I shook my head.

"So, do you want me to go see if he's still there?" he asked after he shoved the gum back into his pocket.

"Yes." I nodded slightly. "That's exactly what I want you to do. Could you go see?"

Now he stood up taller. "Does Luke Skywalker carry a lightsaber? Of course I can. What does he look like?"

"Um . . . he's pretty skinny."

"And not very much hair," said Billie, interrupting. "Like he has no hair in the middle of his head."

I stared at her.

"What?" she asked, pulling her hand away from the top of her own head. "He doesn't."

The kid looked serious. "Okay, you guys wait here. I'll check it out." He disappeared around the corner.

"I thought we weren't talking to strangers," said Billie, watching him go.

"We're not. Unless they seem all right."

She had a dumb smile on her face. "I knew he seemed all right."

Survival Strategy #26:
USE EVERYONE

BILLIE AND ME WERE STILL WAITING FOR
Star Wars Kid to come back. We sat under the gas station awning and watched Tattoo Guy struggle to get
under the truck.

"What wears glass slippers and weighs over four thousand pounds?" I asked.

"What?" asked Billie.

"Cinderelephant."

Billie nodded, distracted. Usually that one got a smile
out of her.

"Why is that guy following us?" she asked.

"He isn't," I said, trying to make the worry leave her
eyes. "He's just hungry for gas station chips or something."

I was a great pretender, but the knot in my stomach told me I couldn't fool myself.

Billie smiled. "So am I."

"You could not possibly be hungry after all those muffins you ate."

I watched the corner, waiting for the kid to come back. But maybe it would be the Spoon Guy instead. My skin felt all crawly.

Then Tattoo Guy stood up and pulled a handkerchief out of his back pocket. As he mopped his forehead with it, his arm muscles rippled surrounded by a barbed wire tattoo. He had so many tattoos, I could barely see plain skin; he did not look even sort of nice. As if he could read minds, he turned and glared at us, and then went back to making clanking sounds underneath his hood.

I stood up.

"Where are you going?" asked Billie, grabbing my hand.

"Nowhere," I said, putting her fingers in between mine. The inside of the cab looked pretty big. Like it was probably big enough for Antonio's whole family in the back.

Tattoo Guy coughed.

Finally Star Wars Kid rode up, his chest puffed out like he was the Jedi Knight on his T-shirt.

"Yep, he's in there. Standing by the magazines. A white shirt, right?"

The Spoon Guy's creepy face appeared in my mind, but I couldn't remember the color of his shirt. I nodded. "I think so."

The kid stuck his hands in his pockets, his bike balanced between his legs. "Welp. What should we do?"

"We?"

"Yep. Now I have to help." He seemed proud of himself.

Tattoo Guy turned the key to the semi. The truck roared to life and then died again just as quickly. He cursed and kicked the door, then walked toward the front of the gas station. I wondered how long he had been trying to fix it.

"I live just right over there." The kid pointed to the apartment buildings. "You wanna come over? You know, until that guy leaves?"

I shook my head.

Billie nodded.

But I couldn't. I couldn't concentrate. Billie and me, we were trapped. It made me want to throw something. Or hit something. Or maybe sit down right here and have a screaming fit like Billie because I was so mad.

I turned to Star Wars Kid. "Go look again."

"I just did."

"I know. Do it again," I demanded. "I need to see if that weird guy left yet."

"But I was just in there—"

"Fine, if you don't want to help us, then go away."

That hurt his feelings. He scrunched up his eyes. "I am helping."

"Please," said Billie, giving me a look.

I hated asking anyone for help. "Fine," I said. "Please?"

"All right, all right." He turned his bike around. "Did anyone ever tell you that you're pretty bossy?" he asked.

Billie nodded.

Whatever. If bossy meant saving us and keeping Billie and me together, then I'd take it.

He turned the corner and was gone. Now it was only me and Billie. The Air Guy, gone. Tattoo Guy, gone. Star Wars Kid, gone.

Billie blew another bubble into the air, then poked it so the tip of her finger was covered in gum.

Above us, the leaves on the trees hung limp and tired, the heat sucking energy from every living thing.

"Hey."

I turned. Star Wars Kid was back. He rode his bike over, scared. "He's coming."

"Who?" He couldn't possibly mean the Spoon Guy.

"What do you mean, who? That guy you told me to

check on. He's coming right now, walking around the side of the building, heading back here. Hurry. Follow me." He headed toward the apartments.

Billie grabbed my hand.

I didn't have one second to plan or think of a better idea, so we followed Star Wars Kid.

He stopped in front of some tall, thick bushes and pushed his bike right in and then ducked behind it, completely hidden. "Come on," he said, pushing branches out of the way and motioning to us. "We'll be safe in here."

Not knowing what else to do, I pushed Billie ahead of me and followed close behind. The branches whipped my face, scratching my cheek like the bush had claws it used as a defense system to keep out branch-breaking kids. From here we had a perfect view of the back side of the gas station. And just in that moment, the Spoon Guy appeared.

"Ouch," said Billie, holding up her foot. "I stepped on something."

"Shh!" said Star Wars Kid. His eyes narrowed and then he smiled, pushing the sweat out of his eyes with his dirty fingers. He probably hadn't had this much fun in weeks. "Be quiet."

We crouched down like Star Wars Kid and waited. To him it was play, but for us it was too real.

Survival Strategy #27:
NEVER TRUST LUKE SKYWALKER

"SEE, I TOLD YOU," STAR WARS KID SAID, pulling back some branches so I could see the Spoon Guy better. He stared into the parking lot with his hands on his hips.

"Come on," said Star Wars Kid, burrowing deeper through the hedges into a small tunnel of branches, just like a beaver making a burrow. "Don't worry about my bike," he said, climbing over it. "It will be safe here. I'll come back and get it later."

Someone had clearly made this secret path, and I had a strong suspicion it was Star Wars Kid. We crawled on our hands and knees through the bushes until we rounded the corner of the apartment building. He stopped and peered out from inside the bush. "Okay, all clear." He did some sort of weird karate roll and popped out onto the sidewalk.

Billie stared after him, and looked not quite sure if she had to do the same thing.

I pushed ahead of her. "Come on, you don't have to do the somersault." I crawled through, stood up, and brushed dirt off my hands and knees.

Billie's face poked out from inside the bush. "But what if I want to?"

"Billie." We didn't have time for karate rolls.

"Here," said Star Wars Kid. "Just tuck your head under like this and then roll." He did another ridiculous roll just to prove he could.

"Billie, we need to go!"

But she wasn't listening. Instead the bushes rustled, a few twigs snapped, and then she sort of flopped out onto the sidewalk, lying on her back.

I pulled her up, and picked a twig out of her hair. "Didn't that hurt?"

She shook her head, her eyes all sparkly. "I did it!"

Star Wars Kid gave her a high five.

"Yeah, good job," I said, glancing around, trying to decide what we should do next.

"Come on," said Star Wars Kid. "You can come to my house. My mom's at work."

"Okay," said Billie, following him down the sidewalk.

"No, hold on. I need to think for a second." This was not how I had planned things. We didn't have room for weird kids and apartment buildings.

Billie looked at me, and for the first time since Dad left us, she seemed to be having fun. "Come on," she said.

"Do you guys like Double Stuf Oreos? I have two whole packages under my bed, and my brother doesn't even know." Star Wars Kid smiled.

"Okay," said Billie.

Billie and me followed him.

"Can we use your phone?" I asked.

He shrugged. "Sure. Do you need to call your mom to pick you up?"

"Something like that."

We were just about to turn another corner when someone behind us roared, "Hey, idiot!"

Three guys, maybe high school age, ran toward us.

Star Wars Kid yelled, "That's my brother and his Darth friends. They hate me!" He sprinted ahead of us. "Run!"

Survival Strategy #28:
OREOS CAN BE DANGEROUS, TOO

NOW, LOST IN A DEN OF IDENTICAL APARTMENT buildings, we crouched behind a Dumpster. I had no idea where we were.

"Billie," I whispered, pulling her close to me. Her bare foot was cherry-Kool-Aid-colored from all the running. She needed a shoe.

"Shh," hissed Star Wars Kid, breathing hard. Panic was smeared across his freckled face like peanut butter. Behind the Dumpster everything smelled like dirty diapers. Star Wars Kid was on lookout, but I couldn't stand staying here a second longer.

"I think they're gone," I said, as I stood up.

"No, get down. Sometimes they just pop out of no-where," he whispered, pulling me back beside him.

Billie was pale again, only this time the crease between her eyebrows looked like it might slice her in two. "Why are they chasing you?" she asked.

Star Wars Kid shrugged. "Because they can."

"But what happens if they catch you?"

He whispered, "You don't want to know."

Billie's eyes got even bigger. I was not going to have her get all terrified just because some random Star Wars Kid was in trouble with his punk brother.

I pulled my hand away from him. "We're leaving."

"Come on," I said to Billie.

"No," he squeaked. "Stop." Sometimes, animals fake it just to get out of a bad situation. Maybe that's what Star Wars Kid was doing now. Why did he care if we stayed with him or not? Had he tricked us just to protect himself from his brother?

I grabbed Billie's hand and walked toward the sidewalk that I thought led back to the gas station. The Spoon Guy had to be gone by now, so we'd just go to the gas station and call Julie.

But Star Wars Kid followed us, creeping along and looking over his shoulder every second. "Okay," he stammered. "Let's go to my house. Come on, it's just around the corner."

"Look," I said, turning around to face him. "I don't

know what's going on with you and your brother, but we're out of it, okay? Just leave us alone."

"But—"

"Seriously. I don't care." I could not worry about some kid I didn't even know.

"But if you're with me, he might not . . ." The puppy dog look was back.

"Might not what?"

He shrugged. "Never mind,"

"Fine. Whatever," I said.

He looked offended, then he mumbled superfast, "It's just he might not pummel me if you guys are witnesses."

His eyes glistened. He actually looked really scared. Maybe he was telling us the truth.

Billie probably believed him already. She patted his hand like she understood everything. It was not my job to protect him. I couldn't get involved in this. My job was to look after my sister.

We walked past an old stairwell, the railing splintered and cracked.

"Here," he said, bounding up the first step. "This is it. This is where I live." He paused and checked underneath the stairs. He took a deep breath. "It's fine. I think they're gone now." He smoothed his Star Wars T-shirt like it gave him courage.

But of course, I could spy faking it from a mile away,

and I could tell it was taking almost every ounce of his self-control to act like everything was fine.

"You need to use the phone, right? Come on, it's just in here." He walked up three more steps and pointed to the door in front of him.

I hesitated. What I should really do was walk back to the gas station and forget about this kid. "What's your name?" I asked.

"Roger."

"I'm Billie," said Billie. She pointed at me. "This is Liberty."

He nodded, but looked anxious. "Come on. The phone's in the kitchen. Hurry."

He opened the door and disappeared inside.

Billie skipped up the step after him.

"Wait," I said, my foot on the bottom step. Sometimes instinct can be tricky. Like is it your brain or your heart telling you not to do something? And right now I couldn't tell which one it was, but—

"What's the number?" he yelled.

"Come on," said Billie, taking me by the hand and leading me upstairs. It would only be for a second, just a phone call to Julie and then we'd wait for her at the gas station. I wondered how many hours it would take for her to drive here. Eight? Ten?

The apartment was dark, and it took my eyes a second

to adjust. Somebody needed to open a window, because it smelled like old sausage.

Billie sat down at the kitchen table. In the center sat a huge ceramic bowl full of Legos, with little partially made cars and ships all over the table. She picked up a Lego guy holding an ax.

"Here," he said, holding the phone out to me. "Oh, that's just some of my stuff I'm working on," he said to Billie.

She looked impressed.

I grabbed the phone. "Thanks." I pulled out my notebook and dialed Julie's cell phone, but instead of a ring, it made a clicking sound, and then a beep.

What was wrong?

Star Wars Kid stared.

"What?" I asked.

"Sorry. Nothing." He turned to the living room. "You guys want to watch TV or something? I have every Star Wars movie. Even the making-of the movies." He pulled out a DVD case.

I shook my head.

What if Julie never answered? Should I call Antonio? I mean, I probably should, but just the thought of his face looking like he knew all along that Dad was a loser made me mad.

Then I tried Julie's home number. The phone rang, and the answering machine picked up. I was half listening when Billie said, "Don't you have some Oreos?"

"Billie," I hissed. "We're not eating here."

But then I got distracted by the phone, and Billie and Star Wars Kid disappeared down the hallway.

I had to leave a message. "Hey!" I yelled. "What's the address here?"

But there was no answer.

I told Julie again that we were sort of near the Grand Canyon and that I'd try to call her back and then I hung up.

"Billie." I went down the hallway. There were three doors, all of them closed.

"Billie!" I yelled, flinging open the first door. It was the bathroom. I opened the next; it was a bedroom all nice and neat with the bed made like it was at a hotel, probably his mom's.

"Billie Marshall, you come here right now!" Blood rushed through my veins. Nothing could happen to her. I was in charge. I had no idea who this kid really was. I put my hand on the doorknob in front of me.

Billie opened the door, her mouth covered in chocolate. She stood in a bedroom with two twin beds. "What?" she asked.

Half the room was covered in Star Wars stuff, and the other side was really messy, with clothes and food wrappers everywhere.

"Why are you screaming my name? I'm right here."

Star Wars Kid stood behind her, holding a package of Double Stuf Oreos. "What's the matter? Was your mom home?"

I wanted to smack the cookies right out of his hand. "She's not allowed back here." I pushed Billie up the hallway, back the way we had come.

"He said I could have another cookie."

"No," I said. "We're leaving."

Star Wars Kid followed me. "I promised her she could have another. Do you want one?" he asked, his mouth creased with black cookie crumbs.

"She can't go anywhere without me, especially into some room with you. We don't even know you," I said so loudly that I sort of even scared myself.

Star Wars Kid stepped back a little and leaned against the wall. "Sorry," he said, shrugging his shoulders. "She just wanted an Oreo."

"Whatever." I spun around and grabbed Billie's arm. "We're leaving." We marched down the hall and turned the corner into the kitchen, where we were startled by a tall kid standing at the front door. Star Wars Kid's brother. The one we were running from.

"What's up," he said, turning his baseball hat backward. He had a nose ring. And he didn't smile. His eyes flitted over Billie and me and then landed right on Star Wars Kid. His eyes narrowed. I could tell he was mean.

I shuddered as my instincts kicked in. Both my mind and my heart were telling me we had to get out of here.

Survival Strategy #29:
DON'T BE A HERO

"GET OUT, JAX," SAID STAR WARS KID. "MOM said you had to leave me alone."

Billie and me backed up so we were now standing right next to him.

Jax didn't look too concerned about his mom. He turned and locked the front door. "Where'd these girls come from?" he asked.

"They're my friends."

Jax laughed. "You don't have any friends."

Star Wars Kid's cheeks turned red. Finally, he whispered, "I do, too."

Jax forced another laugh as cold as the inside of the ice machine at the gas station. "What?" he asked, putting his hand to his ear. "Speak up, numb-nut. I can't hear you."

Star Wars Kid looked down, his nose running. He wiped it on his T-shirt. Snot smeared across the *S* and the *T*.

"We're his friends," said Billie, taking a step forward.

I shook my head, pulling her behind me. Jax exhibited standard predator behavior. If we just stayed still and quiet, he might leave us alone.

"That's impossible." He took a step toward us.

I couldn't stop looking at the locked door—it was getting hard to breathe. Now Jax was standing right in front of us. His T-shirt was wrinkled, like he had slept in it, and his breath smelled like Doritos.

He turned toward Star Wars Kid. "You're a loser. No one wants a loser for a friend." He pointed to Billie. "You need a six-year-old to stand up for you?"

Star Wars Kid looked at his feet. A tear ran down his cheek and plopped onto his tennis shoe. He clutched the package of Oreos in his fist like he was trying to squeeze the cookies to death. The other hand opened and closed like it couldn't decide what to do.

Don't hit him, I thought. There was no way Star Wars Kid could beat up his brother; Jax was almost as tall as Dad.

"Isn't that right?" Jax poked Star Wars Kid in the chest, *hard.* The cookies dropped and Star Wars Kid slumped up against the shelf holding the TV.

"I'm not six, I'm eight," said Billie, poking her head out from behind me.

"Billie!" I whispered, pushing her back. "Be quiet." If we could only get to the front door, then we could run for it. I inched us closer.

Then Jax looked at me, his eyes like those dead fish we saw at the pier the day of Mom's funeral. "Shut your mouth," he said, trying to look around me at Billie.

I stood up taller, staring him in the eyes. *Go away.*

He laughed. "Ohhh. Nice, nice. You think you're tough? I like that." Jax turned back to Star Wars Kid, pushing his face so close that they had to be breathing the same Dorito air. "But this one's a wuss. Who cares about *you*?" he said, and then he spit in Star Wars Kid's face. And for a second, I wasn't sure what happened, because it happened so fast.

Star Wars Kid went crazy—like bearded-dragon, wild-animal crazy. When animals are pushed, they can only take so much before they break. He screamed and jumped on top of his brother, pummeling him with his fists. But Jax's fist smashed Star Wars Kid in the side of the head, and then they were just a mash of arms and legs and teeth and I couldn't tell what was really happening, except that Star Wars Kid was absolutely losing.

"Come on!" I yelled to Billie, pulling her toward the front door.

Billie's eyes were as big as steering wheels. "We have to help him."

I dragged her forward. "No way. Now's our chance." I twisted the dead bolt and pulled open the door. A breeze rushed in, blowing our hair back as we ran down the steps. Even from here I could hear Star Wars Kid crying. For a second, I paused. Billie looked at me, her eyes so full of—what? Hope? Fear? I couldn't tell, but she nodded at me.

"That's right!" Jax yelled. "You little punk, don't you ever—"

And that's when I made my decision. And it seemed like I could almost fly, because I reached the top of the landing in one huge step and pushed open the door.

"Stop it!" I yelled.

But nothing stopped. Jax still pounded Star Wars Kid. Star Wars Kid cried louder. I had to stop it or something bad was going to happen. I remembered Billie's cheek and Dad's hand. I had to stop it.

Then I spied the huge bowl of Legos sitting on the kitchen table. I grabbed it, my hands shaking, and before I could even think or make a plan, I walked over to them. Jax was still on top of his brother. Star Wars Kid's legs kicked out from underneath Jax.

"Leave him alone!" I yelled. But he wouldn't stop. So I threw the bowl as hard as I could. It smashed Jax in the back with a loud thunk. He rolled off of Star Wars Kid. He was stunned or confused. Or maybe both. But for a second, he just lay there, frozen.

"Come on," I said, grabbing Star Wars Kid by the hand.

Billie stared at us from the doorway.

Then Jax staggered up to his feet. And after that, we didn't wait to see what would happen. We just ran like we had the wings of a desert hawk, or special Jedi powers, or adrenaline boosts to our bloodstreams. But whatever it was, we ran like we would never have to stop.

Star Wars Kid led the way, limping and running. "To the bushes!" he yelled.

And for a second I was really glad that I had met that weird kid, because he was a survivor just like us. And maybe we needed one another.

Survival Strategy #30:
GO BACK TO THE BEGINNING

STAR WARS KID'S BIKE WAS STILL IN THE bushes, like nothing had happened at all. But now it felt like everything had changed. He had a huge scratch across the middle of his forehead and it was bleeding.

"Are you okay?" whispered Billie, trying to get comfortable as she squatted and leaned against the apartment building. She had leaves in her hair. Now I knew why Star Wars Kid had to make all these tunnels. This was the only way he could stay safe.

"What?" he asked.

"Your head." Billie pointed.

The blood smeared as he swiped his hand across his forehead. "This? No, I'm good." His face was still red and his curly hair was even crazier, like he had been in a fight with a tiger. Which I guess he kind of had been.

We were supposed to be watching for the Spoon Guy, but all I could do was think about Star Wars Kid.

"Seriously, are you okay?" I asked.

He nodded and shrugged at the same time. "Yeah. I mean, I'm pretty used to it."

Goose bumps covered my arms even though it was hot out. "Aren't you worried your brother is going to find us?" He looked pretty mad when he was getting up after I hit him with the bowl.

"No, Jax has no idea I have this place." Star Wars Kid pulled out a smallish plastic box that had been partially buried in the dirt and opened it. He had all sorts of things in it—Star Wars figures, a flashlight, string, a yo-yo, an unopened Sprite, a used Band-Aid. He picked up some gum and held it out to Billie and me. "Want some?"

We shook our heads. For once, Billie wasn't interested in her stomach. She pulled the army guy she found at the pool out of her pocket and handed it to him. "Here," she said. Star Wars Kid took it without a word and stuck it into his box.

"Why's your brother so mean?" she asked.

Star Wars Kid shrugged and snapped the lid back onto his box. "He's been like that for a while. I usually just stay outside if he's home. Sorry, he's an idiot."

Billie and me didn't say anything. 'Cause what do you say when someone is an idiot and there's nothing you can do about it?

"When's your mom coming?" he asked.

"She's dead," said Billie. I started to shush her, but then it seemed like after everything, we owed him the truth.

He looked confused. "Then who'd you call?"

"My mom's friend," I said.

"Oh."

And it felt sort of awkward crouching there in the bushes with Star Wars Kid. Like we were breathing one another's air juice. I stood up a little—my legs were cramping.

"Our dad left us," said Billie, her voice catching on the last word.

"Billie . . ." But then I stopped. Someone needed to know the truth.

Star Wars Kid nodded. "My dad, too."

"No," said Billie. "He left us at the gas station, but he's probably coming back. Any minute. I bet he's probably looking for us right now." She stared at me with laser beam eyeballs.

I shook my head. "I don't think so."

"He is," she insisted.

"Wait," Star Wars Kid interrupted. "Like, just now? He left you at that gas station?" He pointed toward the parking lot.

It was probably better that he thought that. It sounded so much worse explaining that it was yesterday at a different gas station, hours away. I crawled toward the makeshift exit.

"It's fine. I'm handling it. Just forget it. Thanks for letting us use your phone." I turned to Billie. "Come on."

She inched toward me. "Yeah, and thanks for the cookies. They're my favorite."

"Stop," said Star Wars Kid. "You can't just leave. You need help."

I peered out of our hiding place. The gas station looked the same and the semitruck was there, I guess still broken. Now I wished Billie hadn't said anything. "We're fine. I told you, I called our mom's friend. She's picking us up; she's probably there already waiting for us." I swallowed. Faking it sometimes made my throat hurt.

Star Wars Kid calmed down. "Okay, only if you're sure she's there. But if not, I mean, you can stay with me."

Jax's face floated in my brain. "No, she's on her way."

"All right," he said, picking at the dried snot on his T-shirt. "Let me at least check to make sure that weird guy is gone." He poked his head out of the bushes for a second and then came back in. He smiled with his eyes and did an awkward little bow. "All clear."

It was nice to see that after everything, Star Wars Kid was acting more like himself.

Billie crawled out first, and I started after her when Star Wars Kid put his hand on my shoulder.

"Thanks," he said.

I shrugged. "You would have done it for me."

"Yeah." He put his hand over his heart, crossed his eyes, and flared his nostrils. "May the Force be with you."

"Okay. It will be. Thanks, Star Wa—I mean, Roger." I smiled. It felt good to use his name. He deserved it after everything we had been through. Then I followed Billie out onto the sidewalk.

Roger stayed inside the bushes, but he pushed his fist out of the leaves and pumped it up and down. "Win and conquer!" he yelled.

I laughed. And I pumped mine back at him. I wondered how long it would be before he could go home. Would Jax be there, ready to beat him up again?

"Come on," I said to Billie. "We're going to wait at the gas station." We were getting really good at waiting.

Billie's shoulders slumped, but she followed me anyway.

We walked toward the gas station. The right side was hidden by some trees, but I could see the back wheels of the semi. We were about ready to pass the trees when we heard someone yell, "Hey!"

Billie and me turned.

It was Jax.

He stood on the sidewalk, right in front of Roger's hiding place. Then Jax barreled toward us.

Roger popped up out of the bushes. His head looked like it was floating in a sea of green leaves. "Run!" he yelled.

Jax spun around.

Then Roger jumped out of the bushes and tackled his brother.

Billie and me skittered past the trees and turned the corner. The cab of the semitruck sat with the door wide open, and Tattoo Guy was nowhere in sight.

"Come on," I said, pushing Billie up the steps of the truck. We only had seconds before Jax got away from Roger.

Billie stumbled into the truck with me following close behind.

"Get in the back," I said, pushing her behind the two front seats. We hunched down next to a little pullout table and bench. Except for us, the cab of the semi was empty.

We sat for a minute, and then I crept forward, trying to see out the window. Jax stalked around the parking lot in circles. What had happened to Roger? I shuddered. He had given away his special hiding place just to help us. My heart thumped. It felt good to have a friend, even if it was just for a minute.

Jax looked behind the air pumps, and then he walked toward the truck. He looked underneath and started to walk to the open door when Tattoo Guy rounded the side of the gas station.

"Hey!" he yelled at Jax. "Get away from there!"

Jax jumped. "Bite me," he said, then ran toward the apartment building, disappearing around the side.

Tattoo Guy cursed.

He could not catch us hiding here.

Tattoo Guy slammed the cab door shut.

No, no. Don't close the door. I jumped back to where Billie was crouched. We would sit and wait. As soon as he started working on the engine again, we'd sneak out.

"There's a cat back here," Billie said. "A black-and-white one."

"Be quiet," I whispered. "We don't want the driver to catch us."

Billie nodded.

Just then the cat skittered to the front of the cab, claiming the passenger seat. It glared at me with its bright yellow eyes, its animal instincts on high alert. It was wondering if we were a threat. After a few seconds, the cat curled up into a ball on the seat, its yellow eyes still on me, but it looked more relaxed.

"I love cats," whispered Billie.

"Shh," I said.

The cab kind of jiggled, and then we heard all sorts of slamming and clanging from the engine.

This was our chance. I crept closer to the door, and looked out the window to make sure it was safe.

"What is it doing in here?" asked Billie as she reached two fingers out to the cat. "Come here, pretty kitty. Come here."

"Stop it," I whispered.

We inched closer to the front so I could see out the window.

The cat pretended not to watch us, but it was.

"It's like a camper back here," Billie whispered. "It has a little table and benches and a TV and a sink and a little fridge—"

It reminded me of the first time we got into Dad's camper.

"—and I think there's a bed up there." She pointed toward a ladder that headed over the table. "That's cool."

My heart continued to thud. "Come on, we've got to get out." I put my hand on the door handle, but before I opened it, I checked outside one more time. It sounded like Tattoo Guy was still working on the engine. What if he found us? He could be like Jax or worse.

Just as I reached for the door, I heard footsteps.

"Hurry, he's coming," I said, pushing Billie back toward the table, but even here I felt too exposed. This was not a great hiding spot.

The cat stood up on the passenger seat and meowed.

"Come on," I whispered, pointing to the ladder. I pushed Billie ahead of me. We climbed up the ladder over the table and landed on the bed that was tucked high over the eating area.

The door opened and Tattoo Guy climbed into the front seat, his hands on the steering wheel, all black with grease. He turned the key. The radio came on to some loud, screamy music. The truck rumbled and started to die out like before, but he slammed his foot on something on the floor and the engine came back to life.

"Yes!" he said, hitting the dashboard. The engine continued to roar. Tattoo Guy left the truck rumbling and climbed back down.

No. No. No. We couldn't stay here. Not with the scary-looking Tattoo Guy. For a minute I missed the Lavender Lady and Orson. I inched toward the ladder and swung my leg over, but before I could get down, he climbed back in and closed the door.

We were trapped.

I crawled back up the ladder and scooted Billie and me as far as I could onto the same side of the semi as Tattoo Guy so he couldn't see us if he turned around. I had to formulate a new plan quickly.

Billie grabbed my hand. "What do we do?" she whispered.

Hurry. Hurry. Hurry.

I might burst into a thousand tiny pieces. My heart felt like it was full of moths, their little wings beating against my aorta. I held my hand over my chest. I had to have a plan.

"It's fine," I whispered to Billie. I closed my eyes, begging my brain for some kind of brilliant inspiration. Instinct? Genius? I needed whatever it was that could help keep us safe.

Billie squeezed my hand.

1. We could sneak out wherever he stopped next. At another gas station?
2. Try to call Julie again, but I had no idea if she would ever answer the phone.
3. I would have to call Antonio's mom now. Even if it proved that Dad was everything she'd said.
4. Maybe buy a bus ticket or something.

It was the best I could come up with under these conditions. I reached into my pocket for the bag with our money, just to count it one more time, but it was gone.

Tattoo Guy pulled the truck forward with the music even louder. He must have turned it up.

"Billie, did you see our bag?" I whispered, trying to hide the panic in my voice.

She shook her head.

I felt all over the bed for it, lifting up the dirty-looking pillows. Nothing. I looked out the little baby window on the side of the bed. Maybe it had fallen out of my pocket and landed in the parking lot, but there was nothing.

Did it fall out at Roger's apartment? Or I could have dropped it when we were crawling through the bushes.

The semitruck jerked, hitting something on the road. Tattoo Guy cursed.

"When did you last see our bag?" I whispered to Billie, trying to act like I had everything under control.

"What?" she asked. The music was so loud.

"Do you have our plastic bag? The one with the money?"

She shook her head. Cat hair stuck to her lips. "It was under our table when we were eating breakfast."

And then I remembered I had put it under our table at the hotel. Everything, all that money, sat at our table in the breakfast room. I never even took it to Roger's house.

Something inside me deflated. How could we get anywhere without that money? And if Julie never answered her phone, then how would we get back to our condo? San Diego was a universe away. How could I ever save us now?

Survival Strategy #31:
BEWARE OF SHARKS

"WHAT'S THE MATTER?" ASKED BILLIE.

"Nothing."

My stomach felt like it was full of rocks pressing me down onto the mattress so I might never get up again. We had to have that money.

The cat meowed even louder. It had been sitting at the bottom of the ladder meowing for at least ten minutes. I knew it was trying to tell Tattoo Guy we were here.

"Shut up!" yelled Tattoo Guy.

I pulled Billie closer to me and held my finger to her lips.

She nodded, her stringy hair stuck in her eyelashes. Good Billie. Sweet Billie. When it came down to it, she always did what I said. Or mostly. We were a team. I grabbed her hand, threading her fingers through mine. "It's okay," I whispered. "We're going to be okay. Don't worry."

Billie laid her head on my shoulder and snuggled into me.

The engine roared and the bed shook beneath us. We pulled forward, bumping over potholes in the road.

The cat continued to meow.

"What's wrong?" yelled the Tattoo Guy, his voice carrying back to us over the music and the meowing.

Billie buried her face in my arm and stifled a sneeze. *Shh.*

"I couldn't help it," she whispered.

Of course she couldn't. None of us could help anything.

The cat kept meowing.

Don't you tell him, cat. You keep your meowing to yourself.

Billie and me had a lot of traveling left to do. Migration usually takes a very long time; just ask a flock of geese. It could take months. Whales migrate, too. Sometimes they can be delayed by fishing boats, or changes in water temperature, or a school of sharks.

Sharks aren't always scary like what you see in movies. Back before I was born, Mom swam with sharks. She told me once when I was in fourth grade and was doing a report in science on the nurse shark. It was one of those unusual days when we had her all to ourselves. She took us to my favorite place, the aquarium. I had my face pressed against the glass of the shark tank, which made long, streaky steam marks from my nostrils, but Mom hadn't told me to stop.

We had been staring at the sharks for a while.

"They look kind of scary, huh?" I asked Mom.

She smiled a smile that I didn't recognize. "Oh, some sharks aren't so bad."

"Yeah, until you're face-to-face with one in the ocean," I said.

"I have been face-to-face with one."

"What?" I asked. "When?"

"A long time ago, when I went with your dad to Australia. It was his idea. He said he needed to practice with his underwater camera. So we went, and of course I was being stupid and trying to impress him, so I acted like it was no big deal."

"Weren't you scared?" The sharks darted past, first in one direction and then another, like they couldn't make up their minds.

She turned to me and laughed. "Of course. Wouldn't you be scared?"

I nodded. I mean, those sharks looked pretty decent

now, but I'd seen on *Planet Earth* what sharks did when they were hungry.

"At first it was awful. But after I got used to it, it was awesome. Sand sharks couldn't care less about people," Mom said.

Then she stopped, like she remembered she never talked about my dad. The happy look in her eyes vanished; replaced by the blank one I usually saw if his name was ever mentioned.

"Are we ever going to see Dad again?" I asked.

The sharks in the aquarium seemed to be swimming faster. "Probably not," she said.

"Why?"

"Trust me, Liberty. It's better this way. It's better for everyone. He isn't the same person anymore. He changed."

"How?" I asked.

She tucked a piece of hair behind my ear. "He just did. He has a lot of problems."

"Like what?"

She stared at the sharks as she spoke. "It's hard to explain. The world is too difficult to manage for your father. He is not comfortable in normal life. He's not the same person I met years ago."

I didn't get it. How could someone change so much?

"Like being camouflaged?" I asked. I knew there was a dragonfly that looked like a stick.

She looked unsure. "Sort of." But then she turned her attention back to the sharks. "Besides the nurse shark, which is your favorite?"

Conversation about Dad over.

And since Mom had died, nothing good ever happened anymore. Except for Billie. She was the one good thing. And Mom was right. Dad was like a shark: interesting to look at from far away, but don't get too close or you'll be sorry.

Survival Strategy #32:
DREAMS ARE DANGEROUS, TOO

I SLID THROUGH THE WATER LIKE A dolphin. In the ocean deep, I had goggle eyes. Everything seemed so much clearer than it ever had on land. Here, everything made sense. The fish, the seaweed, the coral, electric and bright, were a part of me. I held the creamy egg carefully, trying not to rip its shell, and dipped down into the black water, touching the sandy bottom just to say I could.

I had a mission. The sea turtle, the one I saw on the beach—I had to find her. I had her fragile egg, the one she left in the sand. She would want it back. Once she realized what I had, she would want it.

She had to want it.

But the turtle swam away and disappeared into a kelp bed; bubbles chased behind her and then popped into nothing. I was alone, except for the egg. I was responsible. How would I ever take care of a baby sea turtle? I wasn't its mother. How could I possibly know what to do?

Survival Strategy #33:
ACCIDENTS HAPPEN

"DRIVER, TEN-FOUR, I SEE YOU ON MY LEFT. I'll back off the hammer. Appreciate the information. Over."

Static forced its way through my brain, pounding and buzzing. My head was killing me.

"Are you awake now?" whispered Billie.

I couldn't have fallen asleep. I was in charge.

"Liberty," Billie whispered.

I rolled over, annoyed at being disturbed. I had been doing something important, but I couldn't remember what now.

"What?"

Billie looked scared. "You were talking in your sleep. You're being too loud."

I sat up and pushed the pillow away from under my head. It smelled like something rotten. Then I remembered everything: waiting at the gas station, Shiny Head, the Lavender Lady, the Spoon Guy, and Roger and his awful brother, Jax. And for some reason, thinking of Roger made me even sadder than I was. And then, of course, there was the lost money. My stomach twisted.

The semi walls swayed around us as we thundered down the road. The garbled radio and the rumble of the engine hurt my ears. I lay flat on the mattress, staring at the plastic ceiling covered with a pattern of little white dots. Worry nibbled on my toes until it found a hole and climbed right into my body. It dove into my bloodstream and traveled through my veins and into my brain, filling my mind with all sorts of horrible thoughts.

1. We can't do it.
2. We'll never get to our condo.
3. Our dad left us.
4. Our mom did, too.
5. Julie doesn't want us.
6. Nobody wants us.

I pulled my notebook out of my pocket and chucked it across the bed. Tears leaked down the side of my face.

"Are you crying?" whispered Billie, her face only inches

from me, her eyes reflecting worry like a mirror. She didn't need to whisper; I could hardly hear anything but the hum of the road, the radio, and the engine bulldozing us ahead.

I flipped over onto my stomach and wiped the tears with the back of my hand. "No. I think it's the cat. It's getting to me. I must have allergies like Mom."

Billie nodded slowly, examining me with her eyes, like she was searching for proof of allergies. The corners of her mouth turned up a little as she pulled back a small curtain over a window along the right side of the wall.

"Look. A window."

But I turned away. I didn't want to look out a window at a road with a name I didn't know, in a place I had never been, that led somewhere with no familiar face to greet us. I hugged my knees into my chest to stop my stomach from clenching up into a tight ball.

"I saw a dead dog by the side of the road when you were asleep," Billie said softly, craning her neck to look at the road behind us. The sun sat in the sky like a helium balloon clinging to a string. I looked at my watch. It said 2:45.

"It didn't even look dead. It looked like it was just taking a nap, except for the blood," she continued.

"Really?" I said, trying to swallow the lump in my throat. I leaned over and pulled Billie into a hug. "I'm sorry." It came out wrong and muffled into the top of her hair. I tried to blink back my tears.

She pushed herself backward to get a look at my face, and then very slowly she placed a small hand on my cheek. "Don't worry. You're good, Liberty."

I shook my head. No. I wasn't. Look at what had happened to us. It was my fault. It had to be.

"Liberty, you're so good." A smile crept into the corners of her mouth and stayed there.

Meow. Meow.

Billie and I both leaned down and peered over the edge of the bed. The cat sat at the foot of the ladder and meowed at us. Thankfully, we were too far for it to jump up. I didn't want to give Tattoo Guy a reason to come up here.

"Shoo!" I whispered, waving my hand.

"Don't," said Billie. "He's just lonely." Her eyes were soft.

Mine used to be like that, too, soft like bunny slippers. But not now. Not after everything. I craned my neck to see if Tattoo Guy was bothered by the meowing. But all I saw was the sleeve of his shirt and his arm covered in swirls and lines and ghostly faces.

"What are you bawling about?" he yelled. For a second it felt like my blood froze right inside my veins, thinking he was talking to us, but he was just talking to the cat. Then his voice got sweet. "Come here, Mr. Sprinkles. Come on now." His voice reminded me of the chocolaty milk that's left over after you eat a bowl of Cocoa Puffs.

"Mr. Sprinkles," he called.

The cat turned in his direction, licking its whiskers.

"Come on, Mr. Sprinkles. Come give me some sugar." He talked to his cat like it was a baby.

Billie covered her mouth with her hand and whispered, "That's silly."

Maybe a guy who named his cat Mr. Sprinkles really couldn't be all that bad.

Suddenly the truck slowed to a stop. Billie held on to me, and I grabbed on to the edge of the wall as we almost rolled right off the bunk. I held on tight. We could have smashed Mr. Sprinkles flat as a stingray.

"Breaker. Breaker. Waterford Driver, what's the slow-down up there?" Tattoo Guy asked. The garbled static from the CB hurt my ears. Soon, another voice filled the cab, low and loud, but I could only make out a few words over Tattoo Guy's music.

The music stopped, along with the giant truck tires. We were at a standstill, which felt strange after constant movement.

"Do what, driver?" Tattoo Guy asked.

The voice came back. "You've got a brake check ahead at your front door, right side. A four-wheel or something turned over, greasy side up. There's junk scattered all over the road. Watch yourself. Use caution."

"Ten-four. Thank you kindly, good neighbor." Then his music came on again. The truck crept forward as slow as a sea slug. The gears clunked as Tattoo Guy slowed the truck down.

Billie and I crawled across the bed toward the window.

"What did he say?" asked Billie.

"Shh," I whispered, since now it was much quieter inside. "There's an accident or something up ahead. On the right." We both crawled to the other window on the right side of the cab.

Billie pulled the curtain back. We craned our necks and pushed our faces against the glass just to get a glimpse of anything. Red and blue lights flashed ahead, but we couldn't see much yet. The truck crawled along and then stopped again.

Tattoo Guy unrolled his window. "Is it bad, officer?" Just hearing the word *officer* made my skin tingle.

"Keep to the left," said a voice. "We've got almost everything off the road, but the camper's still on its side. Be careful at the end on the right, especially with this load. Where you headed?"

"Barstow. Well, I'm dropping this load in Barstow, but I'm stopping in Junction right before."

"All right, be careful when you go through the weigh station there. It's a madhouse."

"Will do," said Tattoo Guy.

My head spun. There was a camper on its side in the middle of the road? My heart, like the truck engine, began to vibrate. What if it was Dad in that accident? What if it was him lying dead on the road? I gripped the handle above the window.

Mr. Sprinkles started meowing again.

"Come here, kitty," said Tattoo Guy. "Yes, we're almost there, don't you worry. You'll love it. I know you will. It's like cat paradise." He continued to talk to his cat as we inched forward.

"What's wrong?" whispered Billie.

I couldn't turn my eyes away from our window. I had to see it for myself. I had to see that camper slammed across the highway. I had to make sure it wasn't ours.

"Nothing. It's just a bad accident. We just have to wait."

"Okay," said Billie, tucking herself deeper into the crease between the mattress and the wall, until I could barely see her body. The mattress was big, the width of the cab.

My heart began to drum, getting louder with each passing minute.

What if it's him? What if it's him?

We inched along. The smell of exhaust was so strong, I longed for the semi to be riding the road again with the wind blowing all foul things away.

And then we were there, slowly rolling past the destruction.

A busted cooler, a camping chair, boxes of cereal scattered along the road, some blankets, a broken radio, along with what looked like napkins, someone's tennis shoe, and then a bunch of other stuff I couldn't identify. Everything tossed across the highway like sand.

"Is that someone's clothes?" Billie asked, pointing to a smashed suitcase, its hinges wrenched off.

I nodded.

"Were there people in the camper?" she asked.

I swallowed. "Probably."

We passed an ambulance. What if someone had died? What if there was a body? I put my hand over Billie's eyes.

"What are you doing?" She shoved my hand away. "I want to see."

"Fine," I said.

Now we could see people. There was another policeman directing cars, and two guys pulled over watching everything like they were watching TV. Three people sat on the side of the road—a man with blood on his face, a woman crying, and a kid standing barefoot. They stared at the road like they couldn't believe that one second they

198

were doing something innocent like playing Go Fish and eating Pringles at their little kitchen table and now they were standing on the highway with all their stuff destroyed. Just like a tornado. Or an earthquake. Or an Explorer, the car that killed my mom.

One minute, things are nice. And then the next, you're standing shoeless in the road with blood running down your face. Instinct tells you to always keep your eyes open. Watch out, 'cause *bam*—that's how fast things can change.

Billie stared out the window, her cheek looking a little less purple than yesterday. Trust me, everything you've ever known can change in a blink.

The gears on the semitruck squealed as we crawled along even slower than before. Then we saw it, the camper: red—not black like Dad's—on its side, the back cracked down the middle like a giant bear had slashed it with an enormous claw. *Slash*, good-bye walls. *Slash*, good-bye window. *Slash*, good-bye locked door that kept you safe at night. The camper lay injured and sad, like it felt bad it was a pathetic excuse for a camper. Like it was just begging to be put out of its misery.

What if Dad was lying out in the middle of the road somewhere with our smashed camper, waiting for an ambulance to come?

So what? Maybe I didn't care. Why should I? He didn't care about us.

My chest felt heavier.

As soon as we passed the camper, the traffic cleared, and we were finally breathing non-exhaust air, our tires hummed down the highway to . . . where did he say we were going? Barstow. And I knew Barstow was in California, because Dad had stopped there to get food and gas on our way out of San Diego. Barstow sounded good. In Barstow we would call Julie again, somehow. But why wouldn't she answer her phone?

I tried not to think about Mom and the Explorer, but I couldn't help it. What if something like that had happened to Julie, too?

Survival Strategy #34:
DON'T HIDE, GO OUTSIDE

"WHERE ARE WE?" WHISPERED BILLIE.

"I don't know," I said, still staring out the window. It was 4:45.

We had driven for a couple hours, and then we pulled off the highway onto a little road that looked like it led nowhere, except to maybe a faraway sandpit. The dust billowed up into huge clouds as we drove. We passed occasional shacks with yards full of leftover stuff like cars, and mattresses, and rusted swing sets. But always the desert surrounded us in every direction. The miles of nothing on every side made my head hurt.

Tattoo Guy parked his truck in front of a house with three faded flamingos in the yard and a huge satellite dish next to the front door. It swayed in the wind, like it wanted to take off and fly away from this dead, dried-up place. Did the house fall from the sky and land here by accident? No one would purposely live here surrounded by brush, cacti, and nothing.

Tattoo Guy took Mr. Sprinkles and went inside the little house.

I counted the flamingos in my head again and again. "When's he coming back?" asked Billie.

I shrugged. It was hot inside the semi. I opened the window near the bed, but the air coming in felt just as hot.

"I'm hungry," said Billie. And even though she had eaten a mountain of food this morning, it was way past time to eat again. "Go look in there," she said, pointing to the little fridge tucked into the side of the semi's cab.

I looked toward the little house again. Still no movement. Suddenly, I saw Mr. Sprinkles dart past the house, chasing something. He ran through the dirt, into the brush, and pounced. I guessed he'd found his dinner. My stomach growled.

"Okay." I inched down the ladder, still nervous. I crept toward the fridge.

Now Billie began to climb down the ladder, too. "I'm thirsty."

I opened the fridge. It smelled like rotten milk. It had old milk, an apple that looked like it had been there for a while, and half a can of cat food.

Billie pushed ahead of me and scrunched up her nose. "What does he eat all day?"

"He must eat out."

She grabbed the apple.

"Doesn't he have anything else to drink?"

I shook my head.

Billie rubbed the apple on her shirt and took a bite. Then she handed it to me and I took a bite. The apple was mushy, but it would have to do.

"I wish we had brought the water bottle," said Billie, wiping sweat off her face with the back of her hand.

I nodded. I wished many more things than that. I opened the cabinet above the fridge hoping he might have something in there and was happily rewarded with half a box of cereal. "Look," I said, shaking the box of Apple Jacks in the air. "One of your favorites."

Billie shrugged. "Are there any water bottles up there?"

"No, but this will keep your mind off of being thirsty." I poured some cereal into her outstretched hand.

She shoved it into her mouth, pieces falling onto the floor.

"Slow down," I said. But I shoved some into my mouth, too, and crunched on the stale rings. It was better than nothing.

After we ate all the cereal, we stood there for a minute, me staring out the window. Staring at nothing.

No people. No houses. Just miles and miles of empty desert.

Finally, Billie said, "What's taking him so long? I need a drink." Beads of sweat covered her forehead.

A line of sweat rolled down my neck. "I don't know."

"What are we going to do?"

"Call Julie again at the next gas station."

"When?" asked Billie, her face red from the heat.

"Whenever we get out of here."

Billie pushed her hair out of her eyes. "It's too hot."

"I know." I saw once on the news in San Diego how a baby was asleep in her car seat and her dad just drove to work instead of taking her to day care because he forgot she was sweet and little and still asleep in his car. It was a hot day, and he just locked the door and went to work without thinking for a minute that he was doing the one thing he couldn't believe he would ever do. And that poor baby died in, like, twenty minutes or something because it was so hot. And that dad, I bet, was never the same again.

After that, how could he be?

I shook the image out of my mind, but it was hard to forget with Billie's face all red and sweaty. Every second felt hotter, like we were being cooked alive. What if we passed out and never woke up?

Finally I said, "Come on. We have to get out of here."
I opened the door farthest away from the house. Hot air rushed in, but it felt so much better than being stuck in the semi.

I stepped onto the dirt and turned to help Billie down the steps. The top step was kind of scary because it was so far away from the second, and the step below it was even scarier because it was even farther.

I held out my arms. "Hold on to me."

She felt so light, like probably how much a baby seal weighed. I set her on the ground; she balanced on one foot. The other, non-flip-flop foot she held up. There was something like black tar smudged across her heel and dried blood near her big toe.

She stumbled and set her bare foot on the ground. "Ouch."

I steadied her as I examined the bottom of her foot. The ground was harder here, with more rocks pointing their edges into the air, like they were trying to protect themselves from something. That's what rocks would do if they were alive.

"Here," I said, taking my shoe off. I didn't know why I hadn't thought of this before. "You wear mine."

"But it's too big."

"I know, but if you tie it really tight then it should be

fine." Her tiny foot jiggled inside my shoe. My foot when I was eight had to have been bigger than hers. I tied the shoelace and made her stand up and walk a few steps. It worked fine.

"That feels so much better," she said. "But what about your foot?"

"I'm okay." Gingerly, I set my bare foot down; the rocks, using their defenses, pricked me. "There," I said. "See, it's perfect. I think my feet are tougher than yours because I'm older."

Billie smiled. "Really? Oh, good."

The semitruck cast a shadow where we stood. The shade and the breeze felt like an unexpected prize at the bottom of a box of cereal. At least out here, we could breathe.

"Are we going in?" Billie stared at the house. It was made of splintered wood, blue and faded, with a fallen-down chain-link fence wrapped around it. A plastic bag, stuck in one of the rungs, flew like a flag.

I shook my head. "No. We'll just wait out here until he comes out, then we'll hurry back into the truck before he sees us."

"Okay."

The house was quiet, but I had a weird feeling, like something was wrong. That crawly feeling climbed up my spinal column. I turned back toward the road. A tumbleweed floated right over the road, then bounced into the desert brush.

Billie linked her fingers through mine and glared at the house. "All we ever do is wait. What's taking so long?"

"I don't know." The sun sat closer to the horizon now. Mr. Sprinkles darted and pounced on something in the brush. What if Tattoo Guy stayed the night? Then what would we do? No—I heard him tell the policeman that he had to deliver his truckload tonight.

Billie sat on the ground and leaned against the truck's gigantic wheel. It was almost two times as tall as she was.

"Where are you?" she whispered into the air. Not a question really, more like a message the wind could wrap up and take to Dad. What if he heard it?

1. Then nothing.
2. He didn't care.

I reached into my back pocket and felt my notebook. It was safe. It reminded me that I could take care of myself and Billie, too.

Except we kind of needed Tattoo Guy to give us a ride to the next gas station or Barstow, whichever came first.

I turned and glared at the house for maybe the millionth time. What was he doing?

"Ewww," said Billie, jumping up from her place in the dirt and backing up into the gigantic semi wheel. "Gross. What *is* that?"

Survival Strategy #35:
BEWARE OF UNEXPECTED GIFTS

"WHAT?" I ASKED.

Mr. Sprinkles was back. This time he sat at Billie's feet, staring up at her face like he wanted something.

Then I spied it. Next to Mr. Sprinkles lay a furry, matted mess. I poked it with my one shoed foot and it didn't move. Dead. A rat, bloody and fat and minus a head. Mr. Sprinkles looked super proud of himself. If he could smile like the Cheshire cat, I knew he would.

"Sick. Why did Mr. Sprinkles do that?" Billie covered her eyes.

I found a stick and poked at the rat, pushing it away from Billie. Then I lifted it and flung it into the desert, so now it was hidden by a little hill.

"There," I said, brushing my hands off on my shorts. "It's gone."

Billie uncovered her eyes and glared at Mr. Sprinkles, who was now licking his paws and whiskers. "You mean cat. Shoo!"

Mr. Sprinkles paused for just a minute and then went back to cleaning himself. I'm sure he had had a delicious dinner.

"It's not Mr. Sprinkles's fault. He just does what cats do. There's something inside him that tells him to chase little animals and eat them. Don't be too hard on him."

"I hate it," she said, her shoulders relaxing a little.

I remembered something Julie had told me once when her cat left a dead bird on her doormat. "Plus, that means Mr. Sprinkles likes you."

"He killed that thing because he likes me?" Billie asked, her eyes wide.

"He killed a rat and gave it to you, like a present. He likes you a whole lot better than he likes me—I didn't get a rat."

Billie shuddered but didn't say anything. She stared at Mr. Sprinkles, who stopped cleaning and brushed up against Billie's leg.

Suddenly, we heard voices from inside the house, loud and angry.

"No. No!" yelled a woman. She sounded like she was

crying and sort of on the verge of having a Billie-like melt-down.

"I won't do it! I changed my mind."

Then I heard a man's voice—it must have been Tat-too Guy's. I couldn't hear what he was saying because he wasn't yelling.

"No. I can't leave them. You're asking me to leave my babies. They need me. They'll die. I won't do it!"

Billie's eyes got as round as onion rings. "Babies," she whispered.

I nodded. "Come on." We crept toward the house. We had to. That lady had said *babies* and *die*. What was Tattoo Guy doing? We crouched underneath the open window, right next to a garden hose that looked chewed and frayed. It barely clung to the faucet with a few twisted threads.

Billie covered her nose. "What's that smell?"

My eyes began to water. Something inside or outside the house smelled like dead things. Or Porta-Potties. Or worse.

Billie made a gagging noise like she was going to throw up. "Pee-eww," she said.

"Billie, don't," I whispered.

"But it smells gross." Billie gripped the ledge and tried to balance on a rock underneath the window so she could see inside, but she was too short.

211

I inched closer. The ledge was splintered and covered with what looked like scratch marks. A Winnie the Pooh sheet hung as a curtain over the holey window screen, flapping in the breeze. A piece with Eeyore's face on it poked through the larger hole each time the wind shifted. I peered through, my eyes trying to adjust to the darkness inside.

"Come on, Sharlee." Tattoo Guy's voice filled the room, but it was soft now—like he was talking to Mr. Sprinkles. "You said you'd come. Mom wants you to be there. This might be your last chance to see her."

The room was empty except for a sofa shoved into the corner and some dishes scattered along the floor. The walls had a couple of framed pictures of a little girl, but that was it. Tattoo Guy walked across the wood floor and leaned against the wall, talking to a woman who must be Sharlee. She was curled up on the couch and something dark sat in her lap. It looked like a cat. Her hands covered her face and her shoulders shook.

"I can't do it. They're my everything. Since Katelyn died, I have no one." She sighed. "They give me great comfort." She turned away from Tattoo Guy and began talking baby talk to the cat in her lap. "You're my princess, aren't you? You're my favorite, and don't you know it?"

Tattoo Guy closed his eyes. He rubbed his face like he was trying to wash it. Finally he said, "Doesn't Mom mean anything to you?" He stared at the thing on Sharlee's lap like he finally smelled something bad, too. "Mom asked me to come and get you. She's worried."

Sharlee's body got real stiff and she sat up straight. "I'm fine," she said, petting the cat.

"Well, at least let me look at your car. You can't live way out here and not have a working car. What if something happened?"

Sharlee shrugged. "Bob comes out here and brings me what I need."

Billie tugged on my shirt. "What is it? Where's the baby?"

I pushed her away. "I don't know." I scanned the room again.

Tattoo Guy's shoulders slumped, like he had lost some sort of fight.

Sharlee sat hard and silent. For a second, all was quiet, except for the wind occasionally flapping the sheet, and for the sound of my heart, and another noise, too. But I couldn't place it. There was background noise, like at the beach, how the ocean is always growling, or how static hisses when you lose a radio station. A sound hummed through the house.

I peered back through the window and noticed how the corners of the room were kind of moving. Dark shapes tumbled over one another.

"All right then, if I can't convince you," said Tattoo Guy.

Sharlee shook her head back and forth.

He reached into his pocket. "Do you have enough money?"

"Lift me up," said Billie, pulling on my shirt again. "It's my turn to see."

I stepped away from the window and crouched down, examining the ground, searching for something.

"What's that noise?" I asked Billie. I peered into the dark hole scratched into the wood paneling. I leaned in closer, and Billie gasped.

Survival Strategy #36:
INSTINCT CAN BE TROUBLE

"LOOK OUT!" SHE SAID. "IT'S A MOUSE!"

I jumped back just in time to see a large rat slink out of the hole and across my feet.

"That is not a mouse." I pushed myself away, my foot suddenly feeling too bare. The rat slunk along the base of the house and disappeared around the corner. Then in that moment I realized what the sound was. Claws, hundreds of them, scratching in between the walls. I stared through the window. Mounds of rats clambered after whatever was in a bowl on the floor.

Then something warm and hairy slid across my bare foot, and I barely stopped the sound that wanted to come out of my mouth. But it was just Mr. Sprinkles coming back to say hello.

Rats. That's what he had been chasing in the brush.

Obviously forgetting he had just killed one, Billie leaned down to pet him. He curled up at her feet, and without hesitation Billie kissed him on top of his head.

"Don't do that," I whispered. "He's got rat germs."

"Why do you think everything has germs?" asked Billie. "He's sweet."

The corners of Mr. Sprinkles's mouth were smudged with brown. My stomach squirmed just thinking of all the rat guts he had torn through. But then again, he was just doing what cats do. Instinct. In theory, rats were supposed to be like dogs as far as friendliness and intelligence, but somehow looking at the nest of them in Sharlee's house gave me the heebie-jeebies.

I took a step closer and pulled myself up to the window ledge to peek inside again.

Tattoo Guy walked toward the front door.

Sharlee still sat on the couch, humming a lullaby and stroking the shape in her lap. Now I knew it was a rat that sat curled in the folds of her skirt, not a cat. She was like the tiger that took care of the piglets just because she had enough love to give to something that wasn't her own.

Tattoo Guy paused at the door. "I'm going to check your car." And then he left.

"No, don't," Sharlee said to the air.

I had noticed an old car sitting on the other side of

the house. Now I could hear the sounds of Tattoo Guy trying to start an engine.

Sharlee still sat. She stared at the rat in her lap like it was the only thing that mattered in the whole wide world. Like she was going to hold tight and never let go. I understood that wanting.

"Come on," I finally said to Billie. "We've got to get back to the truck."

She didn't answer.

I turned. She was gone. And so was Mr. Sprinkles.

"Billie," I hissed. A narrow dirt path worn through the brush led to the back of the house. It was probably a rat trail. "Billie!" I rounded the corner.

And there she was, curled on the ground, moaning, her eyes clenched shut.

Mr. Sprinkles sat near her, meowing.

I ran to her. "What's wrong?"

"It bit me." She raised her hand high above her head.

I looked at Mr. Sprinkles. "I told you to stay away from that cat. Here, let me see." I reached for her hand, but she pulled away.

"No. A rat. It bit me."

My stomach lurched. In sixth grade, my teacher, Mrs. Mortensen, taught us about the Middle Ages, and how just about everyone died from the bubonic plague, a disease carried by fleas living on the rats.

Billie's hand was smeared with blood, and the skin on her index finger looked torn. "Which rat?" I searched the ground. I had to find it. What if it was sick? What if it had the plague? No, not the plague. The plague wasn't around anymore, but what about rabies? That rat could have rabies, or maybe something worse that I didn't even know about. Could you die from a rat bite?

"Over there." She pointed to the brush. "Mr. Sprinkles chased it and had it by its tail. I was trying to get him to set it free, but it bit me."

She stuck her finger in her mouth.

I slapped her hand away. "Don't do that. It's dirty. You don't know what kind of germs that rat has."

Billie's face scrunched up and tears slid down her cheeks. "I don't want germs."

I lugged her into my arms like when she was four years old. "Shh. You're fine."

She hung on to my neck like a baby koala as I staggered toward the side of the house. My legs shook. Just stepping near the rat hole behind the garden hose made my legs feel like they were ready for a fresh bite. I pushed forward so I could see the front of the house. The wind had gotten stronger, pushing tumbleweeds every which way.

Billie cried, swallowing huge gulps of air.

"It's fine. You're fine." But all I could do was picture

rabies running though her bloodstream. I peeked around the corner. Tattoo Guy was underneath the hood of his sister's car, his back toward us. The semi felt as far away as San Diego. I adjusted my grip, but she was slipping. As I took a step forward, a thorn pierced through the skin of my bare foot. I slid Billie to the ground, felt around the bottom of my foot for the thorn, and plucked it out.

Now Tattoo Guy stood up and walked around to the driver's side of the car. He slid into the front seat and tried the engine. It started and then died. He cursed. The wind blew harder, and more tumbleweeds danced across the front yard.

I leaned against the side of the house. Billie cried as I pulled her back into my arms. I was grateful for the wind that swallowed up her sobs and threw them far, far away.

"Shh," I said.

Maybe she was being rat-poisoned this very moment. I couldn't wait any longer. She was on the verge of a freakout, and my arms felt like they might break.

I peeked around the corner again. Tattoo Guy was under the hood. Maybe I should ask him for help. I took a step forward and then I stopped, crouching next to the house. I couldn't do it. He'd be so mad. He'd call the police.

I just had to get back to the truck. Then I could figure out what to do.

"Okay, I'm going to run. Can you run with me?" I set Billie on the ground and grabbed her good hand.

She shook her head.

"Come on, Billie."

That only made her cry harder.

"Remember yesterday, when you were a cheetah? You were so fast. Let's do that again."

"My finger hurts," she wailed.

I covered her mouth with my hand.

"Billie, you can't scream. Not like last night. You have to be quiet." The Spoon Guy's angry face appeared in my mind.

Her eyes swam with tears. They leaked out the sides of her eyes and created muddy streams down her face.

"If I carry you, will you be quiet?"

She nodded.

I wiped my hands on my shorts and heaved her into my arms again. My legs were still shaky, and now my hands were sweaty.

Just then I heard Mr. Sprinkles meowing. There he was, sitting in front of Sharlee's car like he didn't know he was the cause of Billie's rabies plague. He turned and stared at me. Then he went back to meowing. Right now, I hated that cat.

"What's wrong, Mr. Sprinkles?" called Tattoo Guy. His head was still buried in the engine; he didn't even look up.

"Come on," I whispered to Billie.

I lunged toward the semitruck, hoping my mind powers would give me strength.

Don't drop her. Don't drop her.

Something jabbed into my bare foot again. My brain told me to stop and pull it out, but I couldn't. I gritted my teeth and hoped it would be over soon. Each step felt like it required super strength. I willed my adrenaline to kick in, hoping it would surge through my veins, giving me superhuman power.

But with each step my hands slipped. Billie's skin felt like slimy fish scales. I dug my fingernails into her legs. The truck tire loomed in front of me. *If I can just make it to that tire . . .*

"Liberty!" yelled Billie. "You're hurting me. I'm falling."

And just before we reached it, I couldn't hold on anymore. My arms felt like they were cracking into pieces. With my last step, I collapsed.

Billie slammed into the dirt. A cloud of dust billowed up around us like we were in a dream. The dust filled my lungs. For a second, I wished it could hover over us like a cloaking device and camouflage us from whatever would happen next.

Survival Strategy #37:
HELP YOURSELF

AND THEN, AS IF MY MIND POWERS WERE working, the wind continued to howl and swirl around us, creating a dust storm like I had never seen before. Billie screamed, but the wind gobbled it up, turning her voice into nothing but air. Billie's meltdown at the hotel had been bad, but this was ten times worse. Her eyes rolled into the back of her head. Was it the rat bite? Did she have rabies already?

"Billie, stop it!" I shook her, trying to bring her back to me. The dust swirled; I couldn't even see Tattoo Guy or the little house. I shook her harder; my fingers dug into her arms. But still she screamed, as if she didn't even know I was her sister. Like she wasn't even here on this planet, like her body had been taken over by a rat parasite.

I let go of her and wrapped my arms around myself, trying to stop the shaking. I had to be in charge. This was no time for notebooks or facts. Inside my brain a little voice nagged me. *You can't do this alone. Get help.* But I didn't want Tattoo Guy to help me, with his cursing, and his tattoos, and his angry face. No. I could only trust myself.

Instinctively I reached for my notebook and flipped through the pages. Just doing that calmed me. I had to be missing something. I scanned the front yard: the cracked flamingos, the fallen-down fence, the broken car—

The car.

Tattoo Guy had fixed it, hadn't he? The hood was down. He must have gone into the house.

Inside, the seats were barely held together by chewed-up cloth. Springs poked out everywhere. But then I saw the keys sitting on the seat. And before I could talk myself out of it, I knew what to do. I shoved the notebook into my pocket. Sometimes you have to do something you never thought you'd do, just to put everything back together again.

I slid inside. Like the prairie dogs, we would not have a heart attack while we waited for the snake to come.

Survival Strategy #38:
FLEE

MY HEART FLOATED SOMEWHERE NEAR MY epiglottis. I might choke.

I glanced at the front door of the house. It stayed shut.

I imagined Tattoo Guy with his forearms itching to strangle someone. I had to do something. Something had to be done *right now*.

And before I could think it through, I put the key in the car.

I had to.

It was like the car was begging me. Like it needed me to set it free. It needed me to take it and Billie and me away from this dead place that sucked out your life like a lukewarm chocolate shake, if you let it. Just look at

Tattoo Guy's sister—alone on her couch, petting those rats, like she was dead already.

I turned the key. The car wheezed like it was coming back from the grave. But then it died. I turned the key again and the engine stayed on. I had never driven a car, but I had seen Mom do it hundreds of times. It probably wasn't that hard. I pressed the large pedal on the floor. Nothing happened. Then I pressed the pedal on the right and the car whined.

Just in that moment, someone yelled, *"Hey!"*

Tattoo Guy stood in front of the house, his fists clenched. Sharlee stood beside him, a rat on each shoulder.

I pulled the arm on the steering wheel to the letter *D* and slammed my foot onto the pedal and the car leapt forward, right toward them and the house.

Tattoo Guy and Sharlee jumped out of the way. And the rats, too, I bet.

And just like that—*bam!*—I hit the porch rail. My head whipped forward and smashed against the steering wheel.

And then everything got quiet.

Like the world took a deep breath. A breath so long and so soft that for what felt like a long time, everything was still. Like we were at the bottom of the sea. Billie and me floating along, invincible in our turtle shells where nothing could hurt us, not ever.

I reached for Billie. But I forgot, she wasn't there. And all I could think about was Mr. Sprinkles and his stupid meowing. And how if it hadn't been for him and his rats, then Billie wouldn't be sick.

And then it came.

The tectonics. Everything shaking inside me, mixed with an ache inside my heart that might not ever end.

Survival Strategy #39:
SOMETIMES THEY COME BACK

AND THROUGH THE DUST, BEFORE I COULD even question it, I saw him. He was there.

Dad.

I didn't believe it at first. But it was him. He'd found us. Just like the sea turtle swimming thousands of miles, because why would she ever leave her eggs so helpless? Sometimes even nature didn't seem natural, because parents and babies should always be together.

"Are you okay?" he asked, opening the car door.

Nothing hurt except my head. But it didn't matter because he was here at last. And that meant we could go home. We were safe. We were a family.

"Can you hear me?"

I nodded and smiled. At least I hope I smiled, because

I was really happy. And you should always smile when you're happy. Smiling is the one thing animals can't do. Well, except for monkeys. But if you didn't count monkeys, and I'm not saying you shouldn't, that's one trait only we humans have. When you feel something, you should show it. None of that faking stuff, because really it didn't get you anywhere good. I was through with faking it. I was happy.

"Billie," I said.

"I see her. Don't worry." And he pulled me out of the car and laid me on the dirt, which now felt kind of soft and nice. And then I wasn't in the ocean, because there was the sky. Bluish. With little sheep clouds in it. And it felt wrong and familiar all at the same time.

And then, I saw it.

The dragon with the sword through its heart, and a key, and part of a beautiful lady's face. His arm, from wrist until I didn't know where, covered in tattoos. And that was the worst part.

Because now the dream was ruined. I knew the truth. It wasn't Dad.

He hadn't come. And it made me mad that, for a second, I had wanted him to.

Survival Strategy #40:

SOMETIMES HELP COMES FROM A TATTOOED GUY

TATTOO GUY LAID OUT A BLANKET FOR US outside the semitruck. He said it was too hot in there and that Billie needed some air. The wind had gone down, but occasionally little dust tornados would start up here and there. I looked at my watch. It was 6:42. Sharlee had gone back inside because she said we were disrupting her babies.

It had only been ten minutes, and Tattoo Guy still looked like he had seen Bigfoot.

Or maybe a mermaid. Or a UFO (which really wasn't that crazy, since there probably was life on other planets). He kept staring at me like I might disappear if he looked away. And he kept talking about how that fence rail was falling down anyway. And how one more dent in Sharlee's car wouldn't make a difference. He was just trying to be nice.

"Sorry," I said.

He shrugged.

"This hurts," I said, pulling the ice pack away from my forehead. I held it out to him.

"No, you'll be glad you iced it. You've got quite a bump on your head. Just a little longer," he said.

Tattoo Guy had said he'd completed a class in CPR and emergency training because, as a truck driver, sometimes he was the first one on the scene of a road accident. And he liked to know what to do. He said he was prepared for anything. Even still, I didn't think he was too prepared for Billie and me.

I had already told Tattoo Guy mostly everything, about Dad leaving, and calling Julie, and why we had stowed away in his semi.

Right now, Billie was acting normal, except I couldn't be sure. I kept giving her sideways glances, waiting to see if the rat poison would come. But except for the bite, she seemed fine. Her finger looked like it needed stitches, like the time Mom did when she sliced her hand cutting a watermelon.

And anyway, Billie probably had rabies by now, I bet.

At first Billie had been lying on the ground near the semi. Now she was awake and asking for water. She had drunk three bottles. I had drunk one. And Tattoo Guy said he thought she passed out because she was dehydrated, not because of the rat bite. But he did think she needed stitches. And to see a real doctor.

Tattoo Guy picked up the empty water bottles and tossed them into the semi. "It's about time we hit the road." He turned to Billie. "Are you feeling up to it? You're not going to yak in my truck, are you?"

Billie shook her head.

Tattoo Guy didn't know how close he was to the truth. And now, he didn't seem as scary.

"Are you going to call an ambulance?" I asked.

"No. You girls don't need an ambulance, just a good old-fashioned doctor. Since we're out in the middle of nowhere, it would take an ambulance twice the time to get you to a hospital. I'll drive you."

Tattoo Guy pinched the skin in the middle of his forehead like if he didn't, it might split in two.

"So, when did your dad leave you?" he asked, trying to hide the surprise in his voice, but I heard it sitting there, accusing me—like he was thinking, *What kind of kid gets left in the desert by her dad?*

I watched Billie out of the corner of my eye; she still seemed fine, except kind of out of it. I pretended to pay attention to Tattoo Guy's question. Usually I was really good at answering questions, like in school. But my head hurt.

"What?" I asked.

"When did your dad leave?"

His question hung between us like a fragile spider web. I wanted to wave my hands through it and destroy every tiny thread.

"Yesterday."

Finally he asked, "And where were you when—uh—when he didn't come back?"

Billie interrupted. "He left us at the gas station. Liberty said he went to get ice cream. And Mom can't come and get us because she's in the ocean."

"Billie, stop," I said. I turned back to Tattoo Guy. "We were somewhere near Four Corners, I think."

He got a little pale. "Four Corners is hours and hours from here."

I swallowed hard. For a second I wished we were back in the Lavender Lady's car, still huddled on the floor, hidden from everything.

"How far are we from San Diego?" I asked.

"I'd say, with traffic, four or five hours."

I cleared my throat. Still five hours away. I didn't want Tattoo Guy to think he was stuck with us. "Don't worry, Julie will come. We should call her. But I don't think our dad's coming back," I said, my throat suddenly sore and scratchy. I picked at some sticky stuff shaped like a flower on the bottom of my bare foot.

Billie's eyes filled with tears. "I guess I kind of thought that, too."

Finally Tattoo Guy said, "What I want to do right now is get you guys to a doctor." Then he turned toward his sister's house. "I can't vouch for the health of the rat that bit her. My sister doesn't keep her pets in the best of conditions."

"Pets?" I asked.

"She said they were her babies," Billie said. She wiped tears and snot on her arm. It glistened like snail tracks.

"Yeah, something like that," Tattoo Guy said.

He picked me up and put me in the front seat of the semi, and then he lifted Billie up after me. She tried to scoot into my seat as well.

"You can't sit here," I said. "It's not safe. You need to be twelve."

She shook her head. "He already said I could."

Tattoo Guy climbed into the other side of the semi. He held Mr. Sprinkles in one arm like he was holding a baby. He winked, grabbed on to the steering wheel, and dumped the cat onto the floor. Then he tossed me his cell phone. "Call that Julie of yours. Let her know where you're at."

Now the rocks in my stomach returned. Another message for Julie. Where could she be?

"Is your sister coming?" Billie asked, pointing to the little house.

He shook his head. "No. There's not much I can do for her. She refuses to leave. I wish she would change her mind, but she is who she is."

Mr. Sprinkles jumped onto Billie's lap and curled up like he was going to sleep all day.

Tattoo Guy smiled at Billie. "You watch that hand, now. Just keep it up and away from Mr. Sprinkles. What happened to the napkin I gave you?"

"It blew away."

"Wait a second, I think I have something." He bent over, fumbling around under his seat. He pulled out a first aid kit. He flipped the lid open and dug through until he found what he wanted. "Here, let me see your finger."

Billie got up and held out her finger.

Tattoo Guy opened the wrapper to reveal a Band-Aid with four long ends that looked like wings. It reminded me of a butterfly I saw once in a magazine: the leopard lacewing, which lives in Singapore. When the lacewing is a caterpillar, it has huge spiky thorns all over its body, but after it molts, it transforms into one of the most beautiful butterflies I have ever seen. I'd really like to go to Singapore someday just so I could see a leopard lacewing in person.

Tattoo Guy wrapped the Band-Aid wings around Billie's finger, pulling the skin back together. "Does that hurt?"

Billie shook her head.

"Nothing a few stitches won't fix."

The little S shape in between Billie's eyes scrunched tighter. Was Billie going to freak? I waited for the rat demon to come.

"You're not scared of stitches, are you?" asked Tattoo Guy, starting the truck.

Billie nodded.

"Little tiny stitches? That's nothing; look at this." He pulled up the sleeve of his shirt to reveal an ugly, knotted scar. It cascaded over his shoulder like boiling hot lava. "Motorcycle accident. Two years ago," he said, pulling the truck forward. "My right leg looks the same. Let's just say I was pretty lucky that day, and I know it."

Billie nodded, sucking in every word.

"Not everyone is lucky," I said. "We aren't." It just slipped out. I wanted to slurp it back in, but it was too late. I cringed, waiting for the kind of stupidness people say when they are trying to make you not feel sorry for yourself. When Mom died, I heard all sorts of *I'm sorry*s, stuff that sounds completely like faking it.

Tattoo Guy sighed. "Maybe you're right. You girls don't look so lucky right now, do you?"

Surprised, I pointed to Billie. "I don't think she should sit up here with me. It isn't safe."

He smiled and then winked at Billie. "Oh, I think she'll be all right, just this one time. You girls put that seat belt on. We've got to test that luck theory of yours."

The semi headed down the dirt road.

"Knock, knock," said Billie.

I looked over at her, but she was talking to Tattoo Guy.

"Who's there?" he asked.

"Barbie."

"Barbie who?"

"Barbie Q. Chicken!" Billie laughed.

So did Tattoo Guy. "Now, that's a good one." He smiled as he maneuvered the semi over a small hole in the road. He crinkled his brow. "I don't think I know any age-appropriate jokes."

"Do you have kids?" Billie asked.

I pretended like I didn't care, but really I wanted to know the answer. Did Tattoo Guy have some kid somewhere who he ignored and never talked to, just like our dad?

"Me?" Tattoo Guy laughed. "Nope. Not that I know of. I don't think I'm a kid kind of guy."

Billie shrugged her shoulders. "You'd probably be pretty good."

"You think so?" he asked.

Billie nodded.

I pulled my notebook out of my back pocket and flipped through the pages. There it was: the gentoo penguin picture my dad took. I picked at the edge of it and pulled. It tore down the center, giving a satisfying rip. Now all that was left of the penguin were parts of its back, beak, and foot. I ripped off the other side, taking some of the notebook paper with it. How many times had I stared at it, trying to imagine what Dad was doing right at that moment? I scrunched the picture up into a little ball.

"I'm hungry," yelled Billie. She had rolled down the window.

It was dinnertime.

I stuck the crumpled picture into my pocket. "I'm not."

Billie turned and stared at me. "Yes, you are. We haven't eaten anything good all day."

I glared.

The dirt road turned into a gravel one. We passed a beat-up old house, and I saw a flash of orange near the porch. A life vest, the same color as penguin feet, was hooked over the gate, swimming against the breeze.

I leaned over Billie and stuck my head out of the window. The wind whipped my hair into my face.

"What are you doing? You're squishing me," she said, poking me in the side with skinny twig fingers.

I pulled the penguin photo pieces out of my pocket and held them out the window, my heart beating as fast as the semi's wheels were spinning. Then I set them free. They bounced away from each other like an explosion and then disappeared, like they had never existed.

Survival Strategy #41:
DR PEPPER CAN RUIN EVERYTHING

I HAD TRIED DR PEPPER ONCE BEFORE WHEN Billie and me were with Dad. Dad had a whole bunch of Dr Peppers in his camper. A *whole* bunch. Like, thirty maybe. After a couple of weeks, we were parked at a rest stop near Lake Mead in Nevada and Dad was looking between a trail map and his computer and grumbling to himself.

"Dad, can I have a Dr Pepper?" I asked. Billie and me were playing Go Fish for the thousandth time. Go Fish is, like, only fun for the first five times you play. But when we were with Dad, she always wanted to play because I let her win.

Dad didn't say anything.

I guess I could've taken one, but I wasn't really sure about the rules of living with him. We had only been together for a few weeks, so I didn't know. Were we supposed to ask if we wanted anything in the camper? Technically it was his camper, and his stuff, and his food, and his Dr Peppers.

I thought I should ask.

"Hey, Dad," I said a little louder. "Can I have one of your Dr Peppers?"

"Go Fish!" said Billie.

I picked an angelfish.

"Dad," I said.

"What?" He looked up at me like he couldn't quite remember who I was. His eyes were all bloodshot. I didn't think he had slept the night before.

"Can I have a Dr Pepper?"

"Fine," he said, looking back down at his computer. "Quit bugging me." He was always looking at his maps/cameras/magazines and never really looking at us.

Billie shrugged. "My turn again."

I pulled a can out from underneath the sink and flipped it open with a loud hiss. The bubbles burned my nose.

"Do you have any pool sharks?" asked Billie.

I sat down and flipped over my cards. "Go fish."

"No," said Billie. "I saw it. You have one." She grabbed my cards, knocking Dr Pepper all over the camper floor and all over my feet and all over some magazines sitting in a box.

"Oops," said Billie, staring at Dad with a deer-in-headlights look.

"Here," I said, and quickly handed her some paper towels. The soda soaked the table and the floor and everything. "Quick. Before he notices."

But then Dad did notice, and his eyes weren't on his map or his computer, but they were on his magazines, dripping in sugar and carbonation. Soda splashed down the table all over our bare feet.

Dad cursed and slammed his map on top of the counter.

I'd never seen him mad before.

He grabbed Billie by her arm and tossed her up on top of his bed. "Get out of that mess."

I backed up and crouched against the ladder. Duck and cover. Just like the earthquake drill in Mrs. Mortensen's class. He grabbed the box of magazines and began dabbing them with paper towels. He chucked the wet box out the door. It skipped across the ground until it stopped in a wet heap—*poof*—disappearing into a cloud of dust.

He got on his hands and knees, cleaning up the soda, and only then did my heartbeat quit jumping and my breath stop sounding like I had run a mile around the school track.

Billie hid her head under Dad's pillow, crying.

Then Dad stopped mopping up and went outside with his stacks of wet magazines and laid them out on the picnic table, side by side, to dry.

"It was an accident," I said to Billie as I crawled up onto Dad's bed. Like maybe that was an excuse. Like maybe he would understand that eight-year-olds sometimes had accidents. That twelve-year-olds did, too.

"Don't touch my stuff," Dad yelled from outside. He pointed his finger at us through the camper door.

"It was an accident," I said, loud enough for him to hear.

He scowled.

Billie just stared.

"What's wrong with her?" he asked, coming closer to the door.

"Nothing."

Billie's eyes got real big and she hunched down in the pillow. Watching and waiting for something. Maybe still waiting for the Dad we had always wanted.

This is what I should've said to him:

1. What's wrong with *you*?
2. Why did you even come back?

Dad turned away from us and snapped open a map.

That's when I felt it. The stuff we didn't talk about, heating up inside me.

Hot = Me.

Hot = Billie.

Hot = Him.

Everything felt too hot. Like how magma covers the Earth. Superhot. Infinity hot. Over a thousand degrees, I bet. Last year, during sixth grade science, Mrs. Mortensen talked about plate tectonics. I liked that word.

Tec-ton-ics.

Sometimes I said that word over and over again. Sometimes it made me feel better. Mrs. Mortensen said San Diego was on the San Andreas Fault, where two plates banged into one other. An earthquake could happen any minute if the plates moved. Everyone was waiting for the Big One.

But it hadn't happened yet.

So we practiced being safe, just in case. When the bell rang really loud, we got under our desks, or we stood in the doorway, or if we were outside, we had to stay away from trees and electrical lines.

We practiced duck and cover:

1. Crouch down.
2. Head down.
3. Hands over head.
4. Wait for the shaking to stop.

But what were we supposed to do if the Earth cracked open right underneath us? Then what? Mrs. Mortensen never answered that question.

That day, in the camper, we were like the Earth's crust: Billie, me, Dad. And everything we didn't say was hot, just like one-million-degree molten magma. And right then, I could feel the plates moving, slow and soft. Making us bump into one another. I had wanted to whisper to Billie, "Duck and cover."

But it was too late.

Survival Strategy #42:
EAT FOOD

"WHERE'S MY FRIES?" ASKED BILLIE AS SHE tried to search through the bag with her left hand in the cab of the semi. She held her rat-bitten hand high above her like a medal. She had scattered her napkins and burger wrapper all over, but Tattoo Guy didn't seem to care.

He fumbled around in the paper bag in front of him. "Here," he said, placing an envelope of greasy, salty, slightly firm but perfectly soft fries in front of Billie. Drool leaked out of the corner of my mouth and landed on the tabletop in the back of the semi; I quickly wiped it up.

The first thing we did, once we got on the road, was I called Julie, both of her numbers. Her cell phone still made a weird beeping noise, but I left a message on her home phone telling her to call us at Tattoo Guy's number.

After that, Tattoo Guy called a doctor. The doctor lived sort of close to the rat house. And now the doctor was expecting us, and Tattoo Guy had to drop off his truck load before the next day, so we had to hurry, but he said what was wrong with stopping real quick to get something to eat? So hungry Billie had won—with rat spit coursing through her veins, and it seemed to make her especially cranky.

Right now, Billie smiled at him, but not the golden one. Her drink was as big as her head, and I did not see how she was ever going to eat the double cheeseburger she'd ordered.

"That's too much," I said. "You're going to make yourself sick."

She took a huge bite. Sauce dripped down the side of her mouth and rolled under her chin. "Nuh-uh."

"Thatta girl," said Tattoo Guy, patting her on the back. "I like a kid who can eat."

Eat. Consume. Wolf. Gobble.

I was pretty certain it was Billie's burger that taunted my hypothalamus—the part of the brain that controls hunger. Every animal has one. Once, I saw on TV that if you could trick the hypothalamus into believing you were full, then your stomach thought it was true.

But my hypothalamus wouldn't listen to me; it was much too smart to be tricked.

Tattoo Guy shoved a handful of fries into his mouth and swallowed. His Adam's apple bounced, like a wattle on a turkey's neck.

"You sure you don't want anything?"

I shook my head, even though an angry knot formed in my stomach. Plus, my head was killing me.

Shut up, hypothalamus!

I tried to reason with it, reminding it that I had actually eaten this morning. A little. I guess I had been so worried about calling Julie and about getting away from the Spoon Guy that I hadn't really eaten very much.

Tattoo Guy took another gulp from his soda cup. "Well, I have some extras in case you change your mind."

"Here," said Billie, placing an extra hamburger in front of me. "Eat it."

I clasped my hands under the table and tried not to look at the burger. I shook my head. "I'm not hungry. I don't need anyone to buy me food."

"Yes, you do. You lost our money."

Tattoo Guy ignored us, completely engrossed in his

fries. His lips smacked with each new bite of greasy potato perfection.

"I didn't lose it. I know right where it is."

Billie shrugged. "Well, it's still lost even if you know where you lost it."

Smack. Chew. Crack. Slosh.

Survival was such hard work. Even with my head throbbing, all I wanted to do was eat. So I swallowed my pride and picked up the hamburger Tattoo Guy had bought for me and stared at it.

Billie said, "Eat it."

Tattoo Guy had already finished his food and balled up his wrappers. He looked at his watch. "Time's a-wasting."

He stood and walked to the front seat and then tossed the empty bags out the window.

"Shouldn't you throw those in the garbage?" asked Billie.

Tattoo Guy sighed and opened his door to retrieve the bags. "If I'm not careful, you girls are going to make a saint out of me."

Only then, with nobody looking, could I take the first bite.

It was probably the best hamburger I had ever had in my entire life. It felt good to be a carnivore. All the blood in my body rushed to my stomach, and for a second I didn't have to think about Dad or if Julie would ever pick up her phone. I just thought about how it felt to eat. And how nice it was that my stomach had something to do other than complain that it was empty.

Tattoo Guy got behind the wheel and turned the engine on. "Let's roll, ladies. I'm on a deadline. I don't got all day." But he said it with a wink and a smile. Sometimes a smile makes all the difference.

Survival Strategy #43:
TRUST YOUR HEART

"ARE YOU AWAKE?" ASKED BILLIE, SMILING. Her face was too close to mine, and her breath smelled like Froot Loops.

For a second I couldn't remember where I was. Then I did. We were at the hospital. And maybe it was morning.

I nodded, my arm tangled in wires from the IV. The nurse had put it in my vein last night. My head was bandaged, and I was cocooned in a clean whiteness that smelled like summer at the beach. I tried to sit up, but my head hurt like I had been dragged across the desert floor by a coyote. Except coyotes didn't usually drag people.

I lay back down.

Billie leaned over me. She held up her finger, which was

wrapped in white gauze. "Stitches," she said, still standing too close. "I got four stitches and I didn't even cry."

I pushed her back so I could see her better. "That's brave," I said, trying to focus on her face.

She shrugged. "I know." She picked at the gauze around her finger. "I had to get a shot in my finger and one in my arm, but it didn't hurt that bad."

I tried to sit up again. For a second I was dizzy, but then it went away. I squinted at Billie, framed by the bright sun streaming through the window, like a deep sea jellyfish glowing in the ocean deep.

"Are you all better now?" she asked. "We're at the doctor's house."

"I know."

Last night, Tattoo Guy brought us to "the hospital," but it looked just like a house on the outside. He said that's what a hospital looked like out here, where hardly anybody lived.

Now a nurse came in, not the one from last night. Her curly hair was piled on top of her head, and she had a clipboard in her hand. "You're awake," she said. A smile stretched across her face, creating small lines as delicate as a spiderweb. She pulled a chair up to my bed, grabbed my wrist, and fiddled with the needle under my skin. "How are you feeling?"

I pulled my arm away. "Fine."

The room was all white, except for a framed picture of the desert on the wall. The bed I was in was gray metal, and the other bed was white. I was hooked up to a machine that beeped, and my IV arm felt stiff.

"What time is it?" I asked. I couldn't wear my watch with the IV in my arm.

She pulled the clipboard closer to her chest. "Well, let's see. I'd say it's about seven thirty. I'm Doris, Dr. Martinez's nurse." Her teeth were whiter than any other teeth I had ever seen, like perfect little seashells scrubbed clean by a million grains of sand. "Do you have a headache?" she asked, peering at me.

I hesitated.

"It shouldn't be hurting as much as before. The doctor gave you a pretty good painkiller." She took my temperature.

"You hurt your head." Billie clutched my hand and leaned in close so Doris couldn't hear. "Are you really okay?"

The thermometer beeped. Doris wrote something down and then said, "Are you hungry?"

I shook my head.

"Well, you need to eat. Let me see if I can wrangle up some breakfast. I'll be right back."

I held Billie's hand and finally answered her question. "I am. I'm fine, Billie. You don't have to worry."

But her face said that she didn't believe me. I under-stood that worry. Plus, it made me nervous to be around Nurse Doris. Who was in charge of us? Now people could make us do stuff because all they saw were two stupid kids. They didn't know how far we had come. They didn't know what we had been through.

I squeezed her fingers harder. "I promise I'm okay." Her flyaway hair was wet and combed back from her forehead. She smelled like apricots.

"Did you take a shower?"

She nodded. "You can't leave me," she whispered, her eyes glossy.

I couldn't. I wouldn't. She was my baby sea turtle. "I won't." I closed my eyes again, but I reached my hand out and grabbed the ends of her hair, the tips still wet. Then she set something on my stomach. For a second, I didn't even care what it was; my eyes felt so heavy. But I pried them open. My notebook, with a torn cover, sat on my stomach.

"Thank you."

I sat up higher and flipped through the pages until I saw it, the page I hadn't let myself read. I knew it was there, like a gigantic ostrich egg, waiting to be cracked open. The page I hadn't looked at since Dad had picked us up from Julie's.

But I remembered what it said, and I remembered

Mom's long fingers curled over the pencil as she wrote it, maybe six months ago. Mom had just finished a long overnight shift at the hospital. I had just finished watching *Hunter and Hunted*, the episode about killer whales, and I was writing facts about their pods and how they mate for life and how the baby is called a calf, just like a baby cow. And I was wondering if Dad had ever taken pictures of killer whales, when Mom surprised me.

"Can I see your notebook?" Her hair was still in a ponytail from working all night, and she hadn't even changed out of her scrubs. On mornings like this, she usually went straight to bed, but that day she stayed up for a little bit.

I stopped writing midsentence. My pencil was poised over the paper like it was being held by an invisible string.

"Why?"

"Because." She smiled. The corners of her eyes were thick with tired lines.

"Okay."

She took my notebook and flipped through it. She paused at certain pages, read what I had written, and sometimes she smiled. It felt a little weird to watch her read with me standing there. I felt sort of embarrassed.

"I need to pay more attention," she said.

"What?"

She shook her head. "Nothing. It's just, I work too much. I hate it. I'm sorry, Liberty."

"It's fine, Mom. We're fine."

But she didn't know how sometimes I heard her cry when she thought no one was listening. I knew it was hard for Mom to take care of Billie and me all by herself.

Then she turned to the page where I had glued Dad's picture of the penguin with the Cheetos-colored feet. She stopped smiling and stared at it for what felt like a long time. Then she quietly turned the page.

She asked, "Can I have your pencil?"

"What do you want to do?" I only had twenty-four empty pages left. Once I let Billie draw a picture of a dolphin in it and she ripped the page. Really I only liked me to write in my notebook.

"I just want to write something," she said.

Now, I took a deep breath and stared at what she had written I traced her cursive with big loopy *Y*'s.

I love you, Liberty. Trust your intelligent mind, but more importantly trust your heart. Together they will create your best self.

It was almost too hard, this page, with its corners curled and dirty.

I put my hand over my chest, hoping I could somehow stop the hollow feeling that grew inside the longer I sat here looking at it.

With Dad, I had to try to forget the life I had before, otherwise I couldn't bear it.

I pressed my fingertips into the grooves in the paper where Mom's writing had pressed too hard. I read the words again. I didn't see how I could ever be both parts of myself, logical and emotional. Everything felt too horrible, like I would crack open and explode into a million molecules.

Survival Strategy #44:
KNOW WHO
TO TRUST

FOR SOME REASON, THE DOCTOR WORE AN
eye patch.

"Why do you wear that thing?" asked Billie, pointing
to his eye.

"Billie," I said, trying to shush her. "That's rude."

"What?" she asked. "I just want to know."

The doctor smiled. "It's fine. My left eye doesn't work
very well, an old mountain bike injury, so I wear this."

The nurse came in. "Are you finished with your breakfast, Billie? 'Cause we're clearing everything away."

"No," yelled Billie, running out the bedroom door.

The doctor smiled again. People were always amused
by Billie. Somehow, this morning, she wasn't as amusing
to me. My head hurt.

"So, tell me again what happened? I know you told me a little last night, but I want to make sure I have everything straight," Pirate Doctor said. He was right; I had been too tired to explain everything last night, but I had given him Julie's phone numbers.

"I already told you," I said.

The skin around his good eye crinkled. "Come on. Billie told me her part, so I have the basics, but there's more, I know. You might as well get used to telling it, because a police officer is coming by soon, now that you're up."

I ignored my achy head. "No, first we have to call Julie. The truck driver said we could call her first."

Pirate Doctor said, "I called her and left a message."

I lay back down on the bed and covered my eyes. My insides burned like a bonfire. Where was she? Didn't she know we needed her? Didn't she know our dad was crazy?

He held up a little paper cup. "Also, I need you to take this medicine."

I shook my head.

"Well, it's your choice, but if you think you have a headache now, just wait until the painkiller wears off." He jingled the cup of pills.

I sighed and held out my hand.

"Now, that's good. You'll thank me later."

The pills scratched as they went down, and I slopped water all over myself.

"Come on, tell me what happened to your sister."

"The same thing that happened to me. Our dad left us at the gas station and never came back."

His one visible brown eye blinked. "She said that. But why does she have a bruise on her cheek?"

"Ask her," I said. I didn't know why I was protecting Dad. Maybe part of me still thought he was ours, even though he was awful. His blood was my blood, and that counted for something, didn't it?

"She said she fell."

I picked at the corner of the sheet where a thread had come loose. His one good eye bored into me like it was never going to stop searching for the truth. I closed my eyes and focused on the pounding in my cranium. I had always liked that word. *Cranium*. It sounded smart. But inside my head there was Billie's face—no squiggly line between her eyes, no dirty hair or pinched face. Just her golden self. Before everything happened. That's how she should always look. She should.

But I just couldn't tell. Not yet.

"She fell," I said finally, waiting for the Earth to crack open because I was such a big, fat liar. But nothing happened.

Pirate Doctor said, "Hmmmm."

"You can't separate us. We are staying together. Billie and me. Promise."

He paused. "Doctors never make promises."

"I don't care what happens to us, but we have to stay together. I take care of her. She needs me."

"I'm not the one who gets to make that decision, but I'll do what I can. I promise." He smiled, like maybe he meant it.

Survival Strategy #45:
BEWARE OF PRISONERS

AFTER THAT, DORIS SHOWED ME THE SHOWER. And she let me pick through a box of old clothes and shoes that had been donated to the hospital. Billie said she liked her new-old unicorn T-shirt, but I thought it looked too small. And the Junction County Jamboree T-shirt I wore had an itchy tag. But the only other T-shirt was a Big Bird shirt, so, no thank you.

Then someone knocked at the door.

It was a police officer, except this time he had on a uniform and a shiny badge. He said his name was Officer Buck, but that "all the kids" called him Officer B. What kids? Junction felt almost too small to have children.

Officer B wrote down our names, Dad's name, a description of the camper, and our address so he could "sort everything out." Also he had Julie's phone numbers. And he, too, said he would call her. Then he stuck his pen in the spiral binding of his notebook and said, "I sure am going to work hard to help you girls." Then he winked.

I wasn't sure what that wink was supposed to mean. Yes, he would work hard? Or no? Was he just trying to get Billie and me to like him?

Then Officer B said we had to go with him.

Pirate Doctor didn't want us to go because I had a concussion and I was dehydrated and maybe had something-something stress disorder. And Billie had had the first of her rabies shots and tests, but there were more tomorrow. And she was dehydrated, too.

But since, I guess, the police station was only around the corner, Pirate Doctor finally said okay.

The police car was blue. In San Diego they were black and white, like normal. And Billie got to sit in the front, even though she was only eight, because Officer B said the station was real close.

"You sure you don't want anything to drink?" Officer B asked, gesturing to the small red cooler under Billie's feet at the bottom of his squad car. "It's a hot one out here."

"No, thank you." I shifted closer to the inside of the car door.

Billie already had an orange Fanta sitting in between her legs. She took another gigantic drink, and an orange mustache formed above her lip. Then she examined the stitches on her finger. "That stitch right there hurts the most," she said.

"Don't touch it," I said. "It will get infected."

"I'm already infected with rat germs. But the doctor gave me a shot for that." She smiled. "I'm full of rat spit."

"That's the truth," I said. Then I stared out the window at scrubby bushes, desert, and an occasional little baby house. We turned a corner and pulled in front of what looked like the house we had just left, except this one had a handicapped sign in front.

"Where are we?" I asked him.

"The station."

A small sign out front said JUNCTION COUNTY POLICE STATION.

"There are a couple of people who want to interview you girls. We'll be finished lickety-split." He unbuckled his seat belt and opened his door.

Billie turned to me. "What do they want?"

"Just to ask us some questions. It's okay," I said, eyeing the police station again. It didn't seem very threatening, but I couldn't let my guard down.

"You need some help with that?" Officer B asked, gesturing toward the car door.

"I'm fine." I opened it.

Billie had cried this afternoon when he came to take

us to the police station. I told her it was okay and they weren't separating us, but what if they did?

"You girls all set there?" Officer B asked. He held open the door to the police station and a blast of cool air almost froze my sweat. Goose bumps ran up my arms. Humans never do well with extreme climate changes.

We stopped at a desk.

"Hey, Dina," said Officer B.

A lady with huge glasses and even bigger hair smiled at us. Her eyelids were covered in purple and were twice the normal size because of her glasses. She reminded me of an owl. "What do we have here?" she asked.

"Those girls I told you about," he said.

"Hi there," she said to Billie and me.

"Hi," I said, ignoring the do-good smile plastered across her face.

"How's your day been?"

"They're fine," Officer B said. Then he winked again.

He didn't know if we were fine. He didn't know anything. He grabbed some papers off Dina's desk and ambled down the hallway. I hated it when people talked about me like I wasn't even there.

"Come on, girls," he said.

Dina sat back down and said, "If you need anything, just holler."

"Sit here," Officer B said, pointing to a row of plastic

chairs along the wall, right across from a real, live jail cell. "I'll let them know you're here."

Billie sat down and then patted the seat next to her. "You can sit here."

"I know," I said, setting my notebook on my lap.

"Can I look at your notebook?" Billie asked.

I shook my head.

"Why not?"

I shrugged. "It's just a bunch of stuff about animals . . ."

"I know." She sighed, resting the back of her head against the cinder-block wall. "I like animals, too."

Officer B came over again. "Just make yourself at home," he said.

"Okay," said Billie, all cheerful. How come she was acting all happy now? Probably all that orange Fanta dancing through her bloodstream.

How at home could we feel sitting a few yards away from a jail cell? I craned my neck to see. Was there anyone inside? I'd never seen a real jail cell up close, with its solid-steel-to-keep-you-locked-up-forever bars. Someone could slam the door and toss the key. Is that where Dad would go if they found him?

"Is there anyone in there?" I asked, nodding my head toward the jail cell.

Officer B smiled, tapping the handcuffs hanging from his belt. "Not yet, but the day's not over."

Dina walked in. "They're ready for you," she said to Billie and me.

"Aren't you going with us?" I asked Officer B.

Now Billie stopped smiling and her eyes got all big. She linked her fingers through mine.

"Don't worry," Officer B said. "It's just some people from Child Protective Services. They're really nice."

Billie shook her head.

"It's okay," I said. "Come on. We'll do it together and then . . ." And then what? Nothing I said would make her feel better. I wouldn't lie to her, not anymore.

"After you," Officer B said, holding the door open. "You're the boss."

Of course I was, and I'd make sure that it stayed true.

Survival Strategy #46:
BARGAINING IS BEST

I SNEEZED. THE DUST IN THE CONFERENCE room swirled through the sunlight. I swished my hand through the air, making the dust twist and spin. The gray man sitting across the table stared at me with the look I sometimes got from Dad. Like, *Why do you exist?*

I had already told them my story. The safe one, the one where Mom died, where Dad left us, and how Billie and me were taking care of ourselves until Julie came.

"So, that's the whole story?" he asked again.

Gray-shirt-gray-pants-gray-hair-gray-face, sitting in a folding chair against a gray wall. Camouflaged. Like a stick bug. Was that his survival strategy?

The lady sitting next to him, Carla, made a clicking noise with her tongue as she glared at the man. Then she smiled at me. She seemed mostly nice. She flipped open her notebook. "We also have Officer Buck's notes, but we just want to make sure we're not missing anything."

Billie asked, "Do you guys have cookies?"

"I don't, but I can check in a few minutes," Carla said.

Her brown hair, streaked with red, was tied up in a messy bun. Carla tapped her pencil so lightly, I could barely hear it. The rubber eraser bounced . . . bounced . . . bounced.

The door opened and Dina, with her big purple eyelids, walked in with a tray. "Thought the girls might be getting a little snacky," she said, setting the tray down on the table, filled with granola bars, Cheez-Its, and gummy bears.

"Thanks!" said Billie, grabbing a handful of crackers.

"It's from my secret stash," Dina whispered.

"Do you have cookies? I like pink with sprinkles."

Dina turned toward the door. "Let me check and see what we've got in the vending machine."

I wasn't stupid. I knew what this was, even with the Cheez-Its and gummy bears and granola bars. An interrogation. Intimidation.

All animals do it to get what they want. Standard predator behavior.

I stared back at the Gray Guy. His hair hung in greasy clumps around his head. The button-down shirt he wore made it look like *he* had been living in a camper for two months without a normal bathroom, instead of us.

He sniffed real hard and rubbed the end of his nose. Then I saw it: a booger. A small flaky booger hung down from his nostril. Mom called those "bats in a cave." I would not talk to some guy with bats in his cave. The bat fluttered in his left nostril.

"Can you tell us again what happened before you were left at the Jiffy Co. Gas Station? You said earlier that you were spending the summer with your dad," asked Carla.

Billie got real quiet. All I could hear was the crunching of her crackers.

"Yes, I already told you everything."

"You were to stay with him just for the summer?"

I nodded and then I shook my head. Julie had seemed so relieved when he'd come to pick us up. In the beginning I hoped it was for always. In the beginning I would've done anything to make us a family. But not now.

Finally I said, "I don't know."

She flipped through her notebook and asked the Gray Guy, "Did we get ahold of this Julie yet?"

He shook his head. "Just an answering machine. And the cell isn't working."

I cringed. Where was she? What if something bad had happened?

Carla turned back to me and smiled wider. "Really, my

job is to find out what happened before your dad left you guys and also to find out what you've been doing since he left. I think I understand what has happened since he left, except everything's a little hazy on the part right before the gas station. How were you guys getting along?"

The bars from the jail cell flashed in my mind. Would Dad really go there if they found him? What if nothing happened to him? What if they just let us go back with him? Then what would he do?

I hesitated, then started, "We were—"

Billie sniffed. "Our dad went to get ice cream and then . . . and he didn't come back."

The Gray Guy sighed and crossed his gray leg. His foot wiggled back and forth like a fish tail. He didn't care. They were going to separate us, I could see it clearly written across his face. He just wanted to finish his job so he could go home and watch TV.

Carla adjusted her glasses. She looked like she really wanted to help. She cleared her throat. "Did you have an argument?" She flipped through some papers on her clipboard. "It says here that you have a bruised cheek." She looked at Billie, then back at me.

Billie stopped eating.

"How did that happen?"

I held my breath.

Finally, I said, "I'll talk about it without her here," then nodded toward Billie. "And him," I said, pointing at the Gray Guy. "I don't like him."

Carla stared at him.

"What?" he asked.

"Go," she said. "And tell Officer Buck to come and get the sister."

The Gray Guy shrugged and walked out.

"Why can't I stay?" asked Billie, shoving a handful of gummy bears into her mouth. "We're supposed to stick together. That's what you always say."

"We will. Don't worry. It will only be for a few minutes."

Officer B opened the door. "Come on now, Billie. I do believe Dina has wrangled up some cookies for you."

"Okay," said Billie, staring at me with her worried eyes.

I shooed her away. "It's fine. I'll be out in a second. Go eat cookies. Tell Officer B your Barbie joke."

"A Barbie joke? I sure would like to hear that," said Officer B.

"Okay," said Billie as she followed Officer B out of the room.

I turned back to Carla. And right at that exact moment, she tilted her head just so, and it reminded me of Mom.

Carla placed a strand of hair behind her ear, and then as if on command, all the dust particles right above her head began to spin together in the sunlight. I knew it was time.

Instinct was telling me I should trust her.

I tucked my notebook between my leg and the chair. For once, I knew exactly what I was going to say without writing down all the facts first. I just needed to trust my heart, like Mom said.

I closed my eyes and calmed the tectonics in my cranium.

Survival Strategy #47:
BEWARE OF FAULT LINES

BEFORE THE JIFFY CO. DAD, BILLIE, AND me had spent the night at a desert campground surrounded by cacti, and boulders, and not very many people. In fact, I didn't remember seeing anyone that morning except for Dad, who had his photography stuff spread over the little foldout table in the camper. Cameras were laid carefully on one side and prints were stretched out over the other.

"Stay back," he warned, waving me away with his hand. "I'm working."

His eyes were red and puffy. He hadn't slept much at all last night. And I would know, because I hardly slept anymore, either. Nocturnal was how I liked it. That was the only time I could exist without the eyes of Billie watching me. It was the only time the mountains of tectonics that surrounded us when Dad was awake could take a break.

That morning I was trying to be quiet, but I needed to find breakfast for Billie and me without bothering him. We had been parked at this little out-in-the-middle-of-nowhere KOA (Kampgrounds of America) campground for two days, and we were low on supplies. I thought we were somewhere on the border of Arizona and Utah. I crept around the little kitchen, looking in the cupboards for the last box of Pop-Tarts.

"Liberty," Billie whispered. She lay perched on the foldout bed above the kitchen table, right over Dad's head. "I need to go to the bathroom."

"Quiet." Dad didn't like us to use the bathroom in the camper when we were at a campground because sometimes it stunk.

"Okay, just a second," I said. "I'll take you."

Tectonics bubbled underneath. Fault lines crisscrossed our camper.

I took a deep breath. "Dad?"

He ignored me.

"Dad?"

"What?" He stared at me with eyes that could melt someone into magma.

Billie shook her head. She never liked me to talk to him when he was in this kind of mood.

"Nothing," I said.

I opened another cupboard and reached into the very back, the wood rough and splintery, and there I found the last of the Pop-Tarts. I did a silent happy dance behind Dad and raised the box above my head. Pop-Tart Master.

There was only one silvery package left.

Billie stretched her hand out toward me. "Liberty," she whispered. Then she mouthed the word *please*.

Dad slammed his hand on the table. His cameras bounced closer to the edge. One of the lenses he had been cleaning fell to the floor.

Dad cursed. "What do I have to do to get you two to shut up for five minutes?"

Billie shrank down deeper into the blankets. Her eyes were big. I turned my back on those eyes and tried to be quiet as I opened the package. There were two inside, enough to share.

Dad, with his baseball cap pulled down low, hunched over the pieces of his camera, holding a screwdriver in his hand. I put one Pop-Tart behind my back and turned to Billie, holding up the other one, and opened my mouth wide.

275

She mouthed the word *no*.

I started to hand her the other Pop-Tart, the one from behind my back. But before I could, she reached out to grab the one from my mouth. She reached too far and teetered on the edge of the bunk.

Billie's arms flailed, trying to grab anything to keep herself from falling.

I reached out—I tried to save her. "Billie!" I said, clutching her arm, but it was too late. She fell.

Down. Down. Down. Falling seemed to take forever.

She crashed right on top of the table, right on top of Dad. And right on top of all his precious things.

Then everything got fuzzy.

Billie screamed. I screamed. And Dad froze.

But only for a minute. Because it was like tectonics—plates crashing into each other. The Big One.

Only there was no place to duck and cover.

I tried to help, I did—but I slipped on the glass and the pieces poked me through my socks. Broken camera lenses, flashes, and prints scattered all over the dirty floor of the camper.

And in a flash I remembered. Just pieces, at first. The red faces, the tears, and the yelling.

It came back to me like I was watching it on TV.

Real memories, from when I was little.

The lenses crunched under my feet reminding me to save Billie. Because now Dad had her. And he was slapping her. Hard. With each slap I felt like everything inside me shattered. I rebelled against the instinct inside me that told me to run, to save myself first.

I wouldn't run away from Billie. Not ever.

Instead, I dove right into the epicenter, grabbing him around his waist.

Hit me. Dad, hit me.

I bit him as hard as I could on his arm. I tasted blood.

Dad yelled and dropped Billie on top of his broken camera. Then he sank to his knees, breathing really hard. His eyes were red and faraway, like he wasn't even there.

Billie ran to me and I hugged her close. Then I kicked open the camper door and pulled her outside.

Away. Free from all the shaking.

We huddled under a scraggly tree. Duck and cover, just like Mrs. Mortensen had said. Shaking and sweaty, we crouched under that tree waiting for the Earth to right itself.

I wiped the tears from her eyes. Billie's face was red and swollen, like she had been stung by a million bees.

"Can you see me?" I asked.

Billie nodded.

And we stayed there for I don't know how long. Then

a lady came from nowhere and asked us where our mom was. And she wanted to know where we were from. And if everything was all right.

So we went back to our campsite and sat at the picnic table until Dad came out.

He said nothing, except he had to get gas, so get inside the camper because it was time to go.

Survival Strategy #48:
RESCUE YOURSELF

"IS THAT ALL THAT HAPPENED?" ASKED BILLIE, her mouth full of KFC.

We were eating on trays over our beds in the hospital. And Billie and me were the only overnight patients. I guess that's a pretty good thing about staying at an itty-bitty hospital: you get lots of special treatment.

I swirled gravy into my mashed potatoes. A new nurse was on the night shift and kept poking her head around the corner to make sure we didn't need anything.

"And we get to stay here until Dad comes back?" Billie asked.

"I think so. We need to ask Pirate Doctor," I said.

"Good," said Billie. "I like him. He's nice."

That afternoon with Carla, I wouldn't tell her anything

until she promised she'd keep Billie and me together. Then I told her everything. The whole story. Even the bad stuff. No faking it whatsoever.

After dinner, I tried to sleep. But the sheets were stiff and I still couldn't get used to wearing clothes that didn't belong to me. I pulled on the collar of the T-shirt I wore now. I should've picked the larger one, but it was hard to tell how small the shirt really was when the nurse held it up to me, proclaiming it was just my size.

Billie was sleeping in actual pajamas that were in the box of clean used clothes.

I rubbed my arm where the IV had been.

"Why didn't you drink more water?" Pirate Doctor had asked. "Your sister wasn't nearly as dehydrated as you."

"I don't know." And I didn't. I guess when I was protecting Billie all the time, I sort of forgot about myself.

Now I rolled over and stared at her sleeping in the bed beside me. Tonight, she barely even said good night, but she begged Pirate Doctor to sit by her bed until she fell asleep. He told her stories about all the weird diseases he learned about in medical school and what it was like when he went to El Salvador to help kids who didn't have doctors.

I said that, like, a million iguanas lived in El Salvador, combing the jungle floor for fruit and plants. Billie had told me to *shh* when I interrupted him. Usually she liked to listen to me talk about animals, but not tonight.

I rolled over and pulled the sheet off of me. It was too hot and my head hurt.

I stood up and pulled the curtains back. The moon sat high in the cloudless sky, so large and white that it made me squint. Where was our dad? Why didn't he come back? I'm sure Mom knew where he was. Was she up in heaven? I thought, if she was going to be anywhere, she'd be in the ocean, swimming with a pod of dolphins, or splashing through the waves with a huge smile on her face, searching the shore for Billie and me.

I let the curtains go, not wanting to think those thoughts. I liked it better when they stayed in hibernation. But still, they crept out. What would happen now? Would we stay together? What if Billie wanted to stay here in Pirate Doctor's hospital forever? He seemed to maybe want a Billie girl who was shiny gold and sometimes had angel wings. What would happen to me? Who would ever want me, so serious, and plain, and non-shiny?

Billie sighed in her sleep.

I turned toward her and noticed a light shining from underneath the door. My throat was sore with what-if questions; I could barely swallow. When I pushed on it, the door slipped open, everything quiet like the inside of a clamshell.

Pirate Doctor must have been asleep. And maybe the nurse was, too; she hadn't been in for a few hours. I crept forward to the living room / lobby. And there it was: the phone. Suddenly I wanted to use it. I had to try at least one last time before I gave up hope completely. I'd call Julie.

I picked up the receiver, smooth and cold in my hand, and dialed Julie's cell phone number, and expected to hear the weird beeping, when the phone began to ring. And before I could talk myself into hanging up, I heard Julie's voice. Her voice mail for sure . . .

"Hello?"

I hesitated.

"Hello? Liberty, is that you?"

My voice stuck where my heart was, and for a second even my cranium couldn't compute what was happening.

Finally I said, "Julie! It's me." Tears streamed down my face like I had a leak. I couldn't speak, except for what sounded like weird gulping noises.

Then she said, "Liberty? Is that you? I was just in the middle of listening to my messages. Are you okay?"

And then instead of crying, I laughed. And the phone slipped out of my hand because it was covered in snot and tears and sweat. And then Pirate Doctor was there, standing in the doorway. His eyebrows were furrowed, his mouth turned down. He was mad.

No.

He wiped underneath his eye patch. He was sad.

And he let me talk to her until there was nothing else to say. And the heaviness fell away. And for a second I felt like I was glowing and maybe I could fly. Because Julie said she was sorry. Julie didn't know Dad had gotten bad. Julie had been in Guatemala taking care of sick kids. But she was back now.

And she would come get us.

Survival Strategy #49:
MAKE YOUR OWN POD

AFTER ALL THAT GLOWING AND FLOATING, something happened the next day that made me fall back to the Earth's crust.

1. *He* had been found.
2. *He* was back.
3. I could go see him right now, if I wanted.

I put on a different shirt from the used hospital clothing pile. The nurse had washed my other clothes and tennis shoes, so I put on my old shorts, but my shirt was too stained to ever wear again. I pulled my hair back into a ponytail. My face still felt tight and alien because of all the crying I did last night. But for once, it felt nice to be the one who could act crazy. Maybe I didn't have to be in charge all the time.

I pulled the drawstring tight around my waist and tried to focus. But there were too many thoughts in my head at once; my head felt cramped.

Last night on the phone, Julie said she had been away in the jungles of Guatemala working as a nurse and giving kids shots and stuff. It had something to do with the free clinic where she volunteered. And she didn't have electronic communication sometimes, that's why her cell phone made that weird noise when I had tried to call her.

Before she went to Guatemala, she had called Dad and left him a message on his cell phone telling him where she would be and to check in on us. But he never called her back.

She was coming to get us. She said she was five hours away. And she would leave early the next morning.

After I had talked to her, Pirate Doctor got on the phone and gave her the phone number and address of the little hospital and Officer B's phone number, and they talked about other things, but I don't know what because I fell asleep on the living room / reception area couch.

And if that wasn't enough to make my brain feel suffocated, this morning, Pirate Doctor came into our hospital room while we were eating. He said, "I have something important to say." He paused, and his good eye got all twitchy.

"Just say it," I said, because all I could think about was Julie smashed somewhere across the road. Without Julie, what would we do?

Finally he said, "Last night, they found your dad. He's at the police station now."

That was not what I'd expected to hear. Dad left us at the Jiffy Co. Gas Station, and he wasn't coming back. He had disappeared like all those years before, and if he didn't want to be found, then no one would find him.

Sometimes you don't really know how you feel about something until it happens. And right there in that moment, I needed to sit down.

It wasn't fair.

He shouldn't be allowed to come back.

But he was here.

Pirate Doctor asked, "Do you want to see him?"

I shook my head. But then, what was I supposed to do?

"You don't have to," he said.

All I could think about was what had happened three days ago, the morning Dad left us. And no matter how I tried, I couldn't keep the memory away. It was here. Loud and demanding, having a full-on Billie meltdown, forcing me to decide what Billie and me should do.

Survival Strategy #50:
IF YOU CAN,
BE BRAVE

"YOU DON'T HAVE TO GO," PIRATE DOCTOR said again.

I stared at him. I knew that. I knew I didn't *have* to see Dad, but—

"I don't have to go, right?" asked Billie, rubbing her hand along her cheek; you could hardly see a bruise anymore. Now it almost looked like a regular cheek. But that cheek knew what it had been through, and so did Billie.

Nurse Janice took Billie's temperature again. She smelled like Nesquik.

"No," said Pirate Doctor. "You can just stay here with Nurse Janice and me."

"Maybe I should go," I said.

Nurse Janice said to Pirate Doctor, "Old Ben's in room two. I think it's bronchitis."

Pirate Doctor nodded, but his eyes were still on us. "There's no *shoulds* about it. You don't have to go. Officer Buck said they have all the information they need for now."

"I know," I said, trying to wrestle on my shoes.

Billie came over and sat next to me on the bed. She patted my knee. She seemed a lot older than she had a few days ago. Like maybe I didn't always have to protect her, even though I wanted to. Maybe sometimes she could protect me, too.

She asked, "Are you going, Liberty?"

Everyone looked at me. Even Janice stayed for a second to hear.

"I probably should," I said.

"I'm not," said Billie.

She had so wanted him to be a real dad.

"It's your choice," Pirate Doctor said. "But before you go, make sure you finish your breakfast. You don't want to go over there all empty," said Pirate Doctor.

I stared at Billie, and back at Pirate Doctor, and even at Nurse Janice. I thought of Mom in her ocean heaven, and of the Lavender Lady and Orson, and Caterpillar Eyebrows at the shop at the hotel, and Apron Lady in the breakfast room, and Roger in his bush tunnels. And then

I thought of Tattoo Guy and his lonely sister surrounded by rats. And Officer B and Carla, who had promised she would keep Billie and me together. And finally Julie, driving to get us right this minute, and how she would actually be here in a few hours, standing on the steps of this weird little hospital with Pirate Doctor inside.

All of those faces bumped around in my cranium, smiling at me, wishing me well. And instead of pushing my feelings away, I let them come. Happiness from the ends of my hair, all the way down to my toenails. I had people watching out for me, my own mixed-up pod, wanting good things for us.

I was ready to face Dad.

Survival Strategy #51:
FACE IT

"RIGHT THROUGH THAT DOOR," SAID OFFICER B, pointing. "Wait, wait, I got it." He pushed the door open for me. "I'll go in there with you, if you need me."

"All right," I said. So maybe police officers weren't all bad.

Officer B took off his hat—his bald head was bright and glossy. He followed me through the door.

Dad stood up from his folding chair.

He looked the same. But he had on clean clothes, and his hair was combed. And it didn't look like he had stopped eating or anything. I guess I had imagined maybe he couldn't look normal because he had left his two daughters alone at a gas station three days ago, where just about anything could've happened. People shouldn't look normal after something like that. But no, he looked regular.

Except for the handcuffs. Real steel handcuffs. Trapped. He was the prey.

I had sat in this same room with Carla and the Gray Guy about what felt like a million years ago, but it was only yesterday. And of course the table was in the same place, even though it felt like it should be somewhere different.

Officer B walked across the room and sat on the couch. He picked up a magazine and pretended to read, but his eyes peeked over.

"Is this really necessary?" Dad asked Officer B, holding up his wrists. He still seemed normal, except when I got up close, he looked really tired; his eyes were bloodshot, with dark circles underneath. Like he hadn't slept in days.

Good.

Officer B nodded. "It's for everyone's safety. I'm sorry." But he didn't sound very sorry.

Dad sighed and sat down.

I walked over to the other folding chair across the table and sat down, too.

Dad stared at the bandage on my forehead. Then he cleared his throat. "How are you?"

This is what I wanted to say:

1. How do you think I am?
2. I hate you.

But instead I said, "Fine."

"Good," he said. "That's good."

We sat for another minute. Officer B cleared his throat and turned the page of his magazine.

"What happened to your head?" he asked.

"I hit it."

"Does it hurt?"

I nodded. Tears came to my eyes, but I pushed them away. I would not cry in front of him.

"How's Billie?"

I could feel the tectonics. All those questions. All those things never said.

"Fine."

"Good." Dad cleared his throat again.

Crack. Crack. Crack.

Everything inside me might burst into pieces.

I stood up. I couldn't be in this room anymore, staring at his frozen face and eyes, which wouldn't even look at me. Faking it all over the place. "I'm leaving—"

Dad stood. "Wait. Just wait."

I stopped.

"I told the police officer I wanted to see you girls. Obviously Billie isn't here, and that's my fault. So let me talk to you. Just give me a minute." His hands shook even more. "Please."

For a second, things felt different. He had never talked to me like that before, like I was a real person. And when he finally looked at me, I saw something unfamiliar. Was he sorry?

I sat down.

"It just got so crazy," he began. "I mean, everything just got to be too much. You know?" He looked at me, his eyes kind of pleading. "I never thought I'd find myself in this situation. Then, there you were. I thought I could do it. After all this time, I really thought I could. . . ." His voice trailed off. "You get what I'm trying to say?"

He wasn't going to make me feel sorry for him. I would not be his prey. I would not fall victim to obvious pretending. "Officer B said you were sick or something?"

Dad nodded.

"You don't look sick."

He scrunched up his face and sighed. "I know, but I am. I have these, uh, disorders, you know, inside my brain. You know what a disorder is, right?"

"Yes," I said. I couldn't tell if he was making it up. I folded my arms across my chest and tried to pretend I was ice.

"That's why I left in the first place. I have some problems . . . I mean, I've known I have them. It's just, they get worse with stress. And that's why I don't like to be around a lot of people. I shouldn't be around people."

"Then why did Julie let us go with you?"

"I convinced her I was fine. I really thought I was better. I thought I could do this. I wanted to take care of you girls, like I should have years ago. When Julie called and told me what had happened, I thought this was my chance to fix everything. I really wanted to be the dad I should have been. I was feeling healthy. I feel pretty good when I'm on my own program, with no one to answer to or interrupt me." He cleared his throat.

I folded my arms across my chest. I have a talent. A gift, you could say, where I can actually sit in silence for a long time and feel totally normal. I mean, I can sit and not say a word, not even when someone expects me to. It's amazing how much you can learn about someone when you stop talking.

Dad cleared his throat again.

I sat.

Silence really can be your best friend, if you can stand it. Most people can't.

He continued, "I was supposed to see this therapist, but he's a joke. I travel all the time, so it's too difficult. It doesn't help. None of it does." He ran his hands through his hair, like he might pull it out. "What I really like, more than anything, is to be left alone."

He shrugged, now staring off into space. "Every doctor has a different opinion. They say I'm bipolar, borderline narcissistic personality disorder, depressed, anxiety, I have social phobias. I've been diagnosed with a lot of things, but they don't really know. Doctors think they're so smart, but they don't know anything. They don't know anything about me." Now he was breathing hard, like he had been running a race.

I had never heard Dad say this many words in my whole life.

"That's why I left in the first place, years ago. You know your mom. She could handle everything. A job. A house. Kids. Nothing stressed her out; she didn't need me. So I disappeared. Your mom divorced me. She had custody of you kids. She seemed happier that way." He smiled. "Your mom could rule the world."

I held my breath. He was right. Mom was fearless.

"I still don't trust myself," he said. "Not yet. I promise you, when they found me, I was on my way back to get you. I swear, I was driving back to the gas station to get you."

"You were driving back to get us after two days?! You thought we would still be sitting there waiting for you?!"

I couldn't listen to another word.

Dad's bloodshot eyes filled with tears. "I know I need help," he said.

The metal table wobbled. One leg was shorter than the others.

"I'll get help," Dad said. "Maybe it will work this time."

Did he think I was an idiot? I had a brain. A cranium that actually worked very well. Who would leave their own children? I mean, some animals did it, but we were not animals. We were humans. Humans knew better.

"You left us," I said. "Not in a good place. Not in a safe place. At a gas station! You knew you needed help. You could have called Julie."

"I know. I'm sorry. I wasn't in my right mind. It wasn't me—"

I wanted the tectonics to go away forever. Tears ran down my face. "It *was* you! We loved you. We really tried. You hurt Billie and you left us to dry up and blow away. You left us like we were trash."

"It wasn't me," he whispered again.

And so I laid my head on the table and cried like a baby. I cried and cried until I felt really dehydrated. Then I took a sip from the water bottle that sat on the table.

Dad said, "I know. I screwed up, but it wasn't my fault. It wasn't me." He stared at the table, his hands still shaking.

After a while, all I could hear was my own breathing.

"I'm sorry. I'm sorry. I'm sorry," Dad said.

And right there, sitting at that table, I made some important observations.

First, I realized I was all cried out.

Second, Dad wasn't really back. Not yet, maybe not ever.

Third, it didn't matter what he said about what had happened. All that mattered is what I told myself. And I told myself that I was better than all of this.

My conclusion: I'd create a new pod. A strong one. Something filled with Billie and me and love.

The shaking inside me quieted. I sat up and looked at him.

This is how I felt:

1. Tired.
2. Relieved.
3. Sort of hungry.

This is what I noticed:

1. The tectonics were gone.
2. Dad looked old and sad.
3. I was ready to go back to Pirate Doctor's hospital to see Billie.

"They told me Julie's coming," said Dad.

I nodded.

"That's good. A doctor came to see me this morning,

but I have to see a court psychologist." Pirate Doctor's face floated in my brain. "And a judge. They'll decide what's going to happen next."

"Okay," I said.

"I'm going to get myself back together. I promise."

Now I knew how Mom felt all this time.

This was my dad, whether I liked it or not. The good news was that I was a human. And Homo sapiens, in some ways, are much stronger than animals, because we can choose.

And I chose Billie.

Dad sort of smiled at me. "I'm not better. Probably won't be for a little while," he said. "But I think Julie can take care of you, right?" He held out his hand. It was tan and wrinkled.

Dad didn't know anything about what Julie could do. I stretched my hand out toward his and grabbed it. It felt different. Not soft and warm, like Billie's or Mom's. Just different. Maybe I could get used to it. Maybe.

"Did you go to Four Corners?" I asked.

He shook his head. "To be honest, I don't remember."

"How long do you have to stay here?"

"Until I can see the judge."

I imagined Dad sleeping in Officer B's jail cell, and it made me sort of sad to think of him alone. Just like the male killer whale that swims the sea by himself, never to be included in the pod of his whale family.

"Can you ever forgive me?" he asked.

I turned to Officer B, who wasn't even trying to pretend to read the magazine anymore. He watched us like he was watching a movie, his eyebrows raised just a little. I thought of Tattoo Guy, the scars across his arm and leg and what he said about surviving his motorcycle accident.

He had said, *I was pretty lucky that day, and I know it.*

Tattoo Guy was right. Billie and me were lucky too, because we had survived. And still, we had each other.

Dad waited for my answer.

I picked up the water bottle from the table. The sun shone through the plastic, casting a rainbow of colors across the floor. "Maybe," I said. He was, like, my real biological family. His blood ran through my veins. Maybe someday.

I sort of smiled, and this time I didn't feel like I was pretending. One thing I knew for sure: it was time for everything to be real.

I was through with faking it.

Survival Strategy #52:
NEW PODS CAN BE GOLDEN

JULIE WAS AT THE HOSPITAL WHEN I GOT back with Officer B. She had a gallon Ziploc bag full of Guatemalan candy. "Here," she said, shoving the bag into my arms. Then she hugged me like she'd never let me go.

When she finally did, she sat on Pirate Doctor's couch, swinging her foot a million miles a second. But that didn't stop Billie from holding her hand the entire time. I sat on a chair a few feet away from her.

We told her everything, and it was a lot. Sometimes facts can take a while. But I knew it would be even longer if we had to talk about how we felt. And the whole time she just listened, shaking her head every once in a while. She hardly said a word, just wiped tears from her eyes.

When we finished she pointed to a suitcase in the corner.

When Billie and me opened it, it felt like Christmas. Things from home! Everything still smelled like our condo, and some things still smelled like Mom.

When I tried on a pair of shorts and my SeaWorld T-shirt, they were too small.

Julie asked, "Are you sure those aren't Billie's?"

The shorts really were too small.

"I can't believe you've grown this much over the summer," she said, folding them and stacking them into a tidy pile. Julie swore I had grown three inches. But after everything that had happened with Dad, growing taller didn't seem that big of a deal. If you could pry open my rib cage, I'm sure my heart looked different, too. And heart growth is way more important.

After Billie and me changed into our clothes, we went back into the lobby. Billie had on her golden smile and she sat right in between Julie and Pirate Doctor. They were still talking about medical missions and how they wanted to go on others. We were going back to San Diego with Julie. But I couldn't concentrate. When, exactly, did we get to go? And was Julie going to keep us for always?

In some ways it would be hard to go back without the dream of a dad who could save me tucked into the pages of my notebook. But I guess now I didn't need saving. I just needed my sister. And a pod. Someone nice and good who could take care of us, because I couldn't manage everything as well as I thought I could.

Nurse Doris walked into the room. "Stitches in room one."

Pirate Doctor looked up. "Oh, I'm sorry, Doris. You told me that already." He turned to us. "If you'll excuse me, I'll be right back." And he bumped into the door frame as he walked out, which made Billie laugh.

Julie turned to me. "How lucky are we that he was able to help you girls?"

I nodded.

"I can't even begin to comprehend all that has been done for you."

And I couldn't help but think we had done a lot of the helping ourselves, too.

"It's my fault," she said. "I should have never let you girls go. But I had no idea. Your mother told me very little about your dad. She never seemed to want to talk about what had happened between the two of them. She said it was in the past and she didn't want to think about it."

"I don't want to think about it, either," said Billie.

"And when I got the call from the clinic that they

needed someone to fill in for the medical mission to Guatemala, I just jumped on it. I called your dad and left him a voice mail, but he never called me back. I'm so, so sorry."

And I could tell she was sorry. I didn't blame her.

Julie turned to me. "How are you doing?"

"I'm okay."

She looked at me, her eyes all squinty. "Are you really okay? I mean both of you?"

"Yep." I brushed the hair out of my eyes.

Billie nodded.

"Still, I should've called again to check, but I was so busy. I figured you were having a great time. You know, no news is good news . . ." Her voice trailed off.

"Not always," I said.

"Liberty took care of me," said Billie.

"I know she did. She was amazing. You are one amazing girl, Liberty. You remind me of your mom."

My heart bumped.

"Your mom was one of the smartest people I knew."

"Are we going to live with you?" interrupted Billie.

It was the question I was too scared to ask. And right now, I wanted an answer. Facts were always better than guessing.

"We'll have to figure that out with the courts, and the judges, and your dad. I have no idea if your dad has family, but you can't stay with him. Right now, you'll both stay with me," she said.

"Are you going to be our mom now?" Billie asked.

Julie stared out the window. Finally she said, "I never in my life thought I'd be a mother, but I guess . . ." She didn't talk for a minute, then she smiled. "Could you think of me as your youngish aunt? Besides, I could never replace your mom."

Julie wasn't that young. She was even older than Mom. But what she said was true: no one could ever replace our mother.

Billie whispered, "We can add an aunt to our pod, right?"

"What do you think?" I asked.

Billie nodded. "What about Pirate Doctor?"

"And Tattoo Guy and Roger?" I asked Julie. "Do you think we'll see them again?"

She looked like she was thinking hard for a second. Finally she said, "I'd really like to find a way to thank them. I'll talk to Officer Buck to see what we can do."

In life, nothing was ever certain. But I could hope.

I began, "Maybe we could—"

Billie interrupted, "I want ice cream."

Julie said, "I can probably manage that." She turned to me. "What were you saying, Liberty?"

"Nothing."

"Well, are you up for some ice cream? I think we have to stay out here for a few days to get things finalized with your custody, and your dad has a hearing. I have a hotel booked. We can take your stuff over as soon as Dr. Martinez discharges you. Then ice cream? I'm sure we can find some out here. How about it, Liberty? Is that what you want to do?"

No one had asked me what I wanted for a long time. I picked up my notebook and shoved it deep into the suitcase Julie had brought from our condo.

"Yes, yes, yes. Come on, Liberty," said Billie, pulling on my arm.

"Sure," I said.

But something felt undone. I had changed so much this summer that now I felt like a brand-new Liberty species. Finally I said, "There is one thing I want to do before we go back to San Diego."

"Lay it on me," said Julie.

And so I asked. And it sounded both logical and illogical all at the same time, but inside my heart, it felt perfect. Like the two sides of my brain, instinct and logic, could finally agree.

Survival Strategy #53:
CORNERS CAN BE THE MOST IMPORTANT PIECES

IT EXISTED. THE MAP SAID IT DID, BUT TO see it with my own eyes was something else entirely.

Four Corners Monument, Navajoland, USA.

A parking lot surrounded it. The marker looked like a gigantic compass buried in the ground, encircled by concrete. It glinted in the desert sun like a hot penny. Its long arms reached out north, south, east, and west, stretching invisible lines across the parched desert floor, making it known that this place existed: four places in one.

Just like magic.

A small road had brought us here. Well, the road and the car Julie had driven for seven hours had brought us here. Julie paid a fee and pulled into an almost empty parking lot. She said it would be fun, educational even.

I took the concrete steps one at a time.

Four Corners was where we were headed when Dad left us. It seemed to only make sense that if I could reach this destination, to just stand here—four places at the same time—then I knew everything would be all right.

I walked forward and turned my head to the side so I could read the inscription. Words were placed equally on each quarter of the circle: *In freedom here meet four states under God.* The flags of Arizona, Utah, Colorado, and New Mexico snapped in the wind. And then, as if the wind gave me super strength, I hopped, landing perfectly in the center of the circle. Four places at once, defying the laws of science. Stubborn in its existence like Billie and me.

And Dad? I hoped he'd get better, but it didn't matter so much anymore, because I had Billie.

I turned, looking for her.

She was there with Julie, sitting in the shade, unpacking the lunch we had bought at a grocery store, with way too much food because Billie had to have everything. But Julie didn't care.

Billie must have said something funny, because Julie laughed as she took a bite of her sandwich.

"Billie!" I called.

She waved. So did Julie.

"I just told Julie the Barbie joke!" yelled Billie.

And right then, at that exact moment, I just knew. I guess you could say it was instinct, mixed in with a little inspiration. Maybe it was Mom's soul cells, but I knew we were going to be okay, Billie and me. This place felt almost sacred, like if we stayed here long enough, all of us in our exact places, we might just stay shiny and golden forever.

I looked up at the sky. Little white sheep clouds.

Fault lines crisscrossed inside my heart and my head and forged me back together. I was a newer, stronger Liberty. And for now, that was enough.

ACKNOWLEDGMENTS

A BOOK IS NEVER WRITTEN WITHOUT AN endless supply of lovely human beings to help along the way. And so I acknowledge these people for their expertise, love, and support:

Joy Peskin, editor extraordinaire, who remembered two lost sisters and who loved them from the beginning. Thank you for your editing eye, thoughtful advice, and all-around *hoorays* for this book and for me. Thank you to the team at Farrar Straus Giroux Books for Young Readers who made this book excellent in every respect. Thank you to my publisher, Simon Boughton, and copy editor, Kate Hurley. Thank you to Elizabeth H. Clark for the most amazing cover. Thank you, thank you, and thank you again.

Charlotte Sheedy, my wonderful agent, who said yes immediately, and then has ever since cheered and championed this book and me. Thank you. I adore you.

Thank you to Janessa Ransom and Ann Dee Ellis, the smartest reader/writers I have ever met—as well as some downright awesome people. Thank you for reading this book again, and again, and *again*.

And a *huge* thank-you to the talented faculty, staff, and student body at Vermont College of Fine Arts.

My classmates Nicole Griffin, Emily Wing Smith, Corrinne Lewis, and my other Whirligigs, thank you. Everyone needs an intelligent posse of writers as a cheering squad.

My mom and dad, who never said no to books . . . unless I had unhealthily holed myself up for a day with six or seven, in which case they forced me into the daylight to interact with people. Talking to people is important, too. Your love and unfailing support of everything I choose to do means more than you will ever know.

Thank you to Pam White for dropping everything at a moment's notice when I needed you.

Thank you to my siblings: Kim, Terresa, Jack, and Nick, who have given me an endless supply of sibling stuff to write about. And for being the first friends I have loved and cared for.

So grateful to SJ, GC, SA, LG, and LM, for giving my heart a place to live.

And, most importantly, thank you to Adam, who never said no, even when I sounded crazy (which was sometimes a lot).

Grand Junction
COLORADO NAT. MON.
ARCHES NATIONAL PARK
CANYONLANDS NATIONAL PARK
Montrose
Uncompahgre Plateau
BLACK CANYON OF THE GUNNISON NAT. MON.
CURECANTI NAT. REC. AREA
Gunnison
Glenwood Springs
Aspen
Leadville
Boulder
Westminster
Arvada
Lakewood
Golden
Longmont
Durango
Cortez
MESA VERDE NAT. PARK
HOVENWEEP NAT. MON.
Telluride
Silverton
Ouray
Lake City
GREAT SAND DUNES NAT. MON.
Alamosa
Monte Vista
Del Norte
Pagosa Springs
Farmington
Bloomfield
AZTEC RUINS NAT. MON.
CANYON DE CHELLY NATIONAL MONUMENT
CHACO CULTURE N.H.P.
Gallup
Window Rock
HUBBELL TRADING POST N.H.S.
PETRIFIED FOREST NATIONAL PARK
Holbrook
Winslow
Los Alamos
BANDELIER NAT. MON.
Santa Fe
Española
Taos
Rio Rancho
Albuquerque
Los Lunas
Belen
Socorro
EL MORRO NATIONAL MONUMENT
EL MALPAIS NAT. MON.
Grants
SALINAS PUEBLO MISSION N.M.
N E W M E X
C O L O R
Monument Valley
Kayenta
NATURAL BRIDGES NAT. MON.
Blanding
Moab
Green River
Price
Gallo Mts.
Show Low
Springerville
Fort Apache
Magdalena
Quemado